T0293892

FOLK TALES
OF ROCK AND
STONE

WRITTEN AND ILLUSTRATED BY
JENNY MOON

The
History
Press

To Kyla, Shelley, Isla and Eddie

First published 2019

The History Press
97 St George's Place, Cheltenham,
Gloucestershire, GL50 3QB
www.thehistorypress.co.uk

British Library Cataloguing in Publication Data.
A catalogue record for this book is available from the British Library.

ISBN 978 0 7509 9092 9

Typesetting and origination by The History Press
Printed and bound in Great Britain by TJ International Ltd.

CONTENTS

INTRODUCTION

This book is a collection of folk tales that are, in various ways, about rock and stone. Sometimes the rock and stone are central to the tales, sometimes rock and stone is the environment of the story, and a few stories are more about histories or biographies of rock and stone and the manner in which they have been used. Most of the stories are old ones, completely rewritten and, as happens with stories in their passage from person to person, sometimes I have modified them a little to improve the way in which they work. I have mentioned this where it has been done. Four stories in particular are a bit different. I wrote them to serve some of the aims of the book that I mention later in this introduction. They are the tales in Chapter 3: Biographies of Rock and Stone.

On occasion, inspiration to write a story for this book took me by surprise. One day, I saw children skimming stones on the nearby estuary. We joined in and that led to a tale about skimming stones. I also used the content of that story to explore some ideas about how it was to live in a Tudor village. I had done some research on this history for a small book I wrote about a boy living in a Devon village in 1590, who, like many from coastal villages in Devon at that time, sailed a 4,000-mile round trip to fish each summer in Newfoundland (*Moon*, 2017). But that is another story!

I will start by explaining how the book came to be written, then how I went about selecting and collecting tales for it. I should just say here that my use of the word 'story' and the word 'tale' is synonymous.

I have always been interested in stories in all of their forms. In my last job I was fortunate enough to find myself working in a media school in higher education (Bournemouth University) and so it felt relevant to engage in some thinking about what story is and its role in education. In order to think about this, I wrote a book (*Moon*, 2010), a large part of which was an attempt to understand why humans engage in stories – say 'I'll tell you a story,' and people listen.

When I wrote the book, I was already doing some oral storytelling. I have been collecting stories for oral storytelling purposes for over twelve years, and now draw from more than 250 'ready prepared' stories (that does not mean I do not have to 're-learn' them). They are tales I have heard, read and a few stories that I have written. I am very selective about stories for telling. They need to be strong stories with good imagery, and clear beginnings, middles and endings. There are many folk tales that have very good beginnings, mediocre middles and no proper resolutions. They are entertaining or interesting observations that in some place, something has happened and it might happen again. As I said, stories for telling need strong endings. And the stories in this book have been selected with similar criteria in mind.

Then there is the subject matter, rock and stone. I am fascinated by rock and stone. I remember finding my first worked piece of flint when I was a child. I glowed with pride to see it in the local museum. And when we went camping as a family, I loved going to places where we could find fossils. In particular, I remember fossil hunting in Purbeck in Dorset, looking for fossilised wood at Lulworth Cove. I decided I wanted to be an archaeologist and sadly recall the day when my mother announced to me that women did not become archaeologists. Her error possibly changed the direction of my life at that time. However, I have been able to indulge my archaeological interests more recently and have been involved in excavations, experiences from which have found their way into these tales. The excavations I have been involved in, and much of our knowledge of prehistory, concerns work with and on rock and stone. My interests in geology have likewise been furthered by my involvement with the Jurassic Coast initiatives. I am an ambassador for the Jurassic Coast Trust, which supports the World Heritage site. That means that I go to events on geology and on occasions I tell stories at at them. The subject matter is of course rock, stone and the Devon and Dorset coasts, which are pretty rocky. The tale *Jack Tries Smuggling* was written for one such event.

So when a more recent situation occurred, I had a start on thinking about a collection of tales of rock and stone. I was at a 'Beyond the Border' Festival in 2018 at St Donats Arts Centre in South Glamorgan. Lisa Schneidau was promoting her book *Botanical Folk Tales of Britain and Ireland,* newly published by the History Press. I was inspired to write a similar book. What topic? Obviously rock and stone. I met local history commissioning editor Nicola Guy at the History Press stand and things moved on from there. Writing the proposal for the book forced me to think of what I wanted out of the collection of tales that might make it distinctive. They had to be entertaining, vivid and visually interesting in their scene-setting, and they needed to give a picture of the richness of folk tales and the breadth of the subject matter. Rock and stone are the very structures of our Earth, but as Muir (1986) says, 'Stone is something we tend to take for granted.' I wanted the book to also portray some of my enthusiasm for the rocks and stones that we can so easily pass by. So within the stories is information that is intended to enlighten and educate. In some tales this is more obvious than in others. In particular, the section 'Biographies of Stone' carries stories deliberately constructed around geology, archaeology and history.

So maybe after reading some of these tales, the reader will find herself or himself picking up stones and pieces of rock and looking them over, wondering on their stories, what processes of geology contributed to their form, wondering if they had ever been touched by a human being before and who that might have been, in what clothes, and when and what the stories of that rock or stone will be, long into the future after we have left this land. And maybe that reader will, like me, take interesting stones home and will have them sitting in small groups on windowsills to pick up, muse over and imagine.

Finally, a word about my background. I have shifted around in my career. I started in science with a zoology degree, and since then have moved from psychology and counselling to education, health education, and back to education again. I am interested in how people learn, and the relationship of learning to teaching and professional development. I spent time looking at how 'learning from reflection' and critical thinking can help people become more reflective and effectively critical. These topics and others, such as the use of story in education, have taken me to many places world wide to run workshops for higher education teachers and other professionals, including The Football Association.

In my work I have written nine books, all published by Routledge. I always wanted to write fiction. My last degree was an MA in Creative Writing at Plymouth University, a forerunner experience, perhaps, to this book.

ACKNOWLEDGEMENTS

Tales from a Limestone Quarry: I thank John Scott and Karen Mynard for so generously sharing time and these true stories from Beer Quarry Caves. I had heard some of the stories in at least five previous visits to the Quarry Caves, my favourite visitor attraction in the South West.

Two Happenings in the Lives of Beryl and Bill: I would like to thank Bill for telling part of this story at a story event in my house a couple of years ago. In modified form, it was just what I needed for the Lympstone Village Concert that year.

The Tale of the Pinkish Pebble, The Tale of the Flint Stone and *The Ammonite Fossil*: I thank Anthony Cline for looking through these stories in order to check and correct my geological knowledge.

I thank the Jurassic Coast Trust for the inspiration to collect and write tales of rock and stone (and the coast), and the staff of The History Press for bringing the collection into being as a book.

1

STONES: BE THEY MAGICAL OR SPECIAL?

Hold a stone in your hand and you hold a long, long history. In that history, there may be some leftover of magic.

The Game of Pebbles

This is a much-modified version of a story that I heard at a Cardiff storytelling event. After telling it a number of times as I remembered and reconstructed it, and then writing it for two different purposes, I have altered the story so much that it may bear little resemblance to what I first heard. This is the nature of the folk tale. Within the story there are many themes that are common to other folk tales. Writing the story gave me the opportunity to draw on some work I have done recently on the life of poor villagers in Elizabethan England (Moon, 2017). Unfortunately, I cannot recall who was the original storyteller and I have never found the story written down.

Sara lived with her small son, Jed, in the little village of Topscombe. Like others at the time, her cottage was rough and tiny, and to support them both she worked long hours at the big house that owned most of the surrounding land. Jed might well have been closely related to the landlord's son, but the family denied this and cared nothing for the boy, though they allowed Sara to continue to work so long as she never came inside the big house.

One dark November evening, Sara had just come back home. She had been working in the dairy, as was clear from the milk splashes on her clothes. There had been big storms during the day, but now at least, it was quiet. She raked up the fire in the hearth and put more wood on it, then lit the rush lights that gave flickering illumination beyond that of the fire. She set the cauldron of pottage on the tripod over the flames. She had two parsnips to add tonight. Jed was playing on the floor with three round pebbles that he had found yesterday by the stream. He was rolling them across the floor, trying to hit a piece of stick that he had jammed in the hardened earth floor. He scrambled up and showed Sara one of the stones. It was a white pebble with a dull pink marking on it. Sara admired it, kissed him on the head and went back to the pot. Steam rose. A small rye loaf was ready on the table. There was a pat of butter and a bit of rather dry cheese, the usual meal. The fire crackled and Jed was now agitated for his food. Both of them were always hungry.

Sara had just started spooning the pottage into their bowls when a blast of wind howled through the cottage. The rush lights flared then bent. Some went out. The fire flared, then roared and a strange sound rattled the air. The shutters clattered against the cob walls, but then the air was still again. Sara looked round. She tried to ignore what had happened. Then it happened again. More rush lights went out and Jed stood up in alarm. Sara went to the door to look outside. It was a cold night but the air outside was completely still. Stars shone but there was no moon. Outside there was nothing unusual. She came back in, secured the latch and started to walk over to Jed to comfort him. But where was Jed? Two of his pebbles lay where he had been playing, but he was not there. She called him, looked around the cottage, lifted the rough bedding in the corner, went outside, calling. She came in and took a candle around every corner of the cottage, calling, calling ever more desperately. Jed never disappeared. She went out again, this time looking up and down the track, looking into the nearby cottages. No one was about, no sounds, nothing but the hoot of the old owl.

She went back inside and there was Jed on the floor. It was like before, but he was now sucking the three pebbles, licking them voraciously as if they were his favourite food. He had never done that before. She pulled the stones from his mouth and went to hug him with relief, but he pushed her away and grunted. He smelt odd. Then he grabbed one of the stones from her hand, the white one, and held onto it, resisting her attempts to wrest it from him.

'Jed, my love, thought you was lost ...'

He pushed her away again and when his eyes met hers, there was a hard glare like never before. It seemed to go right through her. This was not like her usual loving child. No hugs and kisses. He must be ill – or – maybe very, very hungry. She went back to the pot on the fire and finished filling the bowls. Jed pushed his away, the stew slopping on the floor. She tried to feed him with the wooden spoon, but he ran around the room stamping and waving his arms.

It went on like that. With difficulty, she put him to bed but he kept getting up and running round. And he would not let go

13

of the stone. At dawn Sara wrapped him up and took him with her as usual. She was doing the milking today. Holding onto Jed, she had made ready the milking stool beside the first cow when Jed pulled away from her, clambered under the cow and started suckling directly from the cow's udder. The cow looked round and lowed in surprise. Sara pulled Jed away in horror and Jed gave her that strange glare. The stone was still gripped in his hand.

After the quick suckle of milk, Jed pulled Sara's shawl around himself, lay on the floor of the dairy and slept while Sara got on with her work.

When Sara finished work that evening, she took Jed to Marlie. Marlie was the woman from whom everyone sought advice. She lived across the fields in a hovel under the hill. She always knew what to do. Marlie opened the door, pulling her ragged wrap up to her neck.

She looked at Sara and the child for a few seconds in silence then she said, 'You have trouble, girl. I can see. Come in.' She pushed back her grey plait and held out her hand. 'Come in – and the boy.'

Jed hung back, refusing to be drawn in by Sara. He kept holding up the white pebble and he only entered when Marlie took him by her rough hand. And then he wandered around inside, apparently fascinated by the containers that lined the walls of the cottage. There were jars of potions and lotions and powders, pots of liquid, bundles of tree bark, bunches of herbs hanging from the beams. On the walls, there were strange black markings drawn in thick strokes in charcoal and chalk. He looked at them, poked at the symbols, jabbing at a particular one, tapping his stone on the symbol. Then he picked up a large spurtle, waved it in a circular movement on the floor and stood in the circle he had drawn, stood quietly for a moment, then stepped out. The old woman watched his behaviour and then showed Sara to the bench.

'What happened?' asked Marlie.

Sara told her how Jed looked exactly like her child but seemed so different. And if this was not her child, where was her Jed?

'This could be a changeling,' said Marlie. 'We'll need to see. It happens when *they* get restless. They've been restless lately – the Others. It's the November storms, and there are troubles at the big house. That's what's upsetting them.' She paused. 'You had things to do with the big house. The boy, I think … '

Sara looked down. 'The Others are restless?' she said. Everyone knew about the Others, but normally you did not speak of them. 'If this is not my Jed, how do I get Jed back?'

Jed hung back, refusing to be drawn in by Sara.

'Course you want him back, my dear. We must bide our time and do this carefully. Be back on the morrow.' Marlie was showing them to the door. 'I see the stone he has,' she said as they went out.

Sara struggled through the next day. In desperation she had let the boy suckle from the cow and, like the first day, he settled, still clutching the stone. In the evening they crossed the fields again to Marlie's cottage. Near her hovel there was a strange sweet smell that seemed to excite the boy. He went straight in and danced round a black pot hanging over the fire.

'Watch,' Marlie said. She lifted the lid of the pot. Steam rose and filled the hovel. It whisked this way and that in the draughts. There were streaks of brown and green steam and that strange sweet smell. Sara reeled back but the boy walked towards it and picked up a wooden ladle. He seemed desperate to drink from the pot. Marlie pulled him back. He wriggled free and she gripped his arm more tightly.

'He is from the Others,' she said. 'This is their favourite food and he is hungry. You can feed him on this.'

She ladled brown liquid into a wooden bowl. The child jumped in wild excitement. She gave him one spoonful. He grabbed for more but she held it away from him and he seemed to calm.

'He is a changeling,' she said. 'Sometimes we can reverse this. Only sometimes. Go home. Feed him this in early evening. He will sleep for a night and a day and we must hope that he drops the stone. Four hours after sunset, or when the stone drops from his hand, leave the boy, but take the stone with you. He will go on sleeping. Go to the rock stack by Dingymoor lake and leave the stone at the foot of the rocks. Climb into the stack and wait to see what you will see. Do not move until whatever you see is gone and come back to me tomorrow.'

The boy did sleep and at last the stone dropped from his hand. Sara pulled her ragged shawl round her shoulders and with the stone in her hand, she walked the dark lanes to Dingymoor lake. Recent storms had brought trees down across the track and several times she had to climb through branches. The flame of her candle threatened to die but glimpses of moonlight helped. Ahead, the rocks were silhouetted against the sky. She left the stone at their foot. She had played there as a child and remembered the way up. With a view of the lake, she waited, shivering in the night cold.

As the moon emerged again from cloud there was a sound, like the strings of a harp played by the breeze. It sung out clearly then was more muffled. The tone made Sara sleepy. When she opened her eyes, there were hundreds of them in the glade by the lake, under the rocks. They were dressed in all shades of green and turquoise, small men and women: the Others. Sara had heard many stories but never had seen them, but anyone would have known. They were dancing gracefully to the music of a small band of players who were strumming on instruments like harps and blowing silver pipes. Near the water, around ten pretty ponies grazed. Then all of the dancers turned to look at the track. A woman rode up on a white horse. Her pale gowns swathed the body of the horse. Her head was held high and whitish hair flowed down her back. Sara tried not to tremble, tried not to move. The leader turned in her saddle. Walking behind her was a group of Others and in the midst of them, though dressed like them, was someone who was different – his skin whiter, his head bigger and his hair. It was Jed, dressed like the Others, walking with the Others, then joining in the dancing like the Others and he looked very happy. They danced around the rocks in which Sara hid. Her muscles ached, cramped, and cold seeped in but still she did not move.

Then a beam of moonlight cast across Jed and immediately the Others drew towards him and stroked his hair. He smiled happily, laughing.

Sara so wanted to call out, run to him, but she did not. It was hard, and harder still when suddenly a mist rose over the lake and drifted into the glade and she could see no more. When it cleared there was nothing but the water and the land, and the grass in the glade was untrampled. Dew glistened in the moonlight. When Sara climbed down the rocks, though, the stone had gone.

Back at home the Other child still slept. Next day after work, Sara took him back to Marlie.

'I saw him, Marlie. I saw Jed with the Others – as if he had been with them all his life. But how do we get him back?'

'Listen carefully,' said Marlie. 'Take a pure white hen – white – not a speck of another colour, mind. Roast it on your fire. The boy will be interested. Let him watch but keep him away. Let the feathers singe, let the fat drip and collect it in a pot. Roast the bird until the flesh is dried. Put the bones outside your cottage. Cool the grease and in the hours after midnight, smear it on the boy's head, then all over him. They may then come and get him. Ask me no more.'

Marlie seemed exhausted and sunk back inside, closing the door on them.

Back in her cottage, Sara drew a slate from the wall under which were hidden a few coins and she went in search of a white chicken. The boy followed her but made no sound. Her neighbours were keen to sell her hens and she saw white bird after white bird only to find a feather here or there that was brown or cream. She was nearly in despair when the boy himself darted to the back of a hen house and brought out a small, pure white hen.

Sara paid and made the hen ready for cooking. She set up a spit over her fire and began to turn it and for hour after hour she turned the spit. The feathers singed and withered. Sharp smoke filled the cottage, stinging her eyes. Then juices and fats started to drip. The boy would have reached to dip his finger into the fat but constantly she held him back. Daylight went. She lit the rush lights and went on turning the spit. The boy started to fight her, kicking and screaming, trying to get to the pot. Then suddenly he seemed exhausted. Sara was exhausted too but now it seemed that she could hear things, beings leaping in the fire, unfamiliar shadows dancing on the walls. The smoke that curled up as the fat spat into the flames seemed to carve shapes in the air.

It felt it was the right time. Shaking deeply, Sara moved across to the door and put the carcass outside. Then she set aside the pot of grease to cool. The child had crept to a corner and now slept. The air seemed thick with moving things, but Sara could see little through the tears in her sore eyes. She lifted the sleeping child and smeared the grease on his head. He woke, then seemed to purr. He clawed at her, wanting more and more of the grease on him. As she smeared on the last of it, she heard the musical sound that she had heard before at Dingymoor lake. It stopped and there was the sound of a strong gust of wind. Dying ashes blew about inside, shutters banged and rattled. The boy stood. Instinctively Sara ran out into the yard to check for damage to her thatch, but nothing moved in the blackness. Nothing had moved and nothing was there. But when she went back in, it was all different. It was as if the air of the cottage had been spring-cleaned. It was clear and fresh. The smoke and smells had gone. Through the cracks in the shutters there were the first streaks of dawn. And standing in a thin beam of light, by the remains of the fire was Jed, so much the same as the Other child, but yet so different. He was yawning and rubbing his eyes. He ran to her.

'Mumma, mumma.'

Sara held out her arms and hugged him. He held out to her the three pebbles. The white one was replaced by a brown pebble. The Other was completely gone, and with him all signs of chicken and grease. As for Jed, all that seemed left from his time with the Others was a vague dream of laughing and dancing and a kind lady with long hair who rode a white horse.

Finding Peace of Mind

This story was inspired by a Yugoslav folk tale retold by Paula Crimmens in a groupwork session for older adults (Crimmens 1998). Over its journey through the many times I have told the story, it has transformed and is more or less a new tale. I still tell the original sometimes but treat it as a different story. Watching how stories evolve is always an interesting process.

Many generations of grandparents ago, there was a small village called Carasov on the shore of the warm blue Mediterranean Sea. On the land side, Carasov was surrounded by dry craggy mountains with just a few trees and scrub on their lower slopes, and olive and citrus down near the village. Goats grazed among the olives together with the donkeys when they were not pulling carts. There were a few fields of corn and a little wheat and small patches of green vegetables. Several fishing boats were pulled up on the stony beach. People were good at fishing in the clear waters.

Generally, Carasov was a happy village. People laughed and talked as they bartered, bought and sold at the market. They moved among the baskets of red tomatoes, yellow peppers and the green leaves of spinach. There were rolls and rounds of cheese, dried sausages hanging up, eggs and creels of fresh fish. There was a stall of multi-coloured woven skirts and shawls for special occasions and always the girl selling ribbons. This was what it was like usually.

When the market had been cleared on the market day nearest to the full moon, a meeting was held in the large hut by the marketplace to deal with village matters. Elders, dressed in traditional robes, would manage the discussion of the next feast day, the fayre, trade with other villages along the coast, the state of the fishing, the goats, the crops, the olives and the occasional disputes between neighbours, though usually these were rare.

But one early summer, things were not so good. Winter weather had dragged on into a soggy spring. Storms washed the newly planted seeds out of the ground so they had to be planted again, and seeds were expensive. A fishing boat was wrecked and three of the five fishing boats left had rotten planks that needed to be replaced, so few fish were landed. There had been little for sale in the market for a while. People were tired of the cold and wet and sometimes they felt hungry. No one remembered it being as bad as this in their lifetimes. They grumbled and complained and became fed up with each other, and at the meeting they were fed up with the elders because all they reported on were the disasters. After a particularly negative speech, a man stood up, looked all round and said, 'We need no more words like yours. Things are bad, we know that. We need cleverness. We need more peace of mind so we can be wise and make things better. There's no peace here now.'

People nodded and clapped. The Chief Elder stood, unsure whether this was criticism of him or not.

'It seems that people agree with you, Perov. So how do you suggest we gain more of this peace of mind you talk about?'

Elders were meant to sort things out.

There was silence then slow murmuring. The elders turned to talk among themselves and people started to drift away, grumbling again. Then a young girl clapped her hands for attention.

'We can't go on like this. There's not enough food for my family. Can't we go and learn to gain peace of mind in the Great City? With the teachers and the tall spires there must be the knowledge we need there. We could bring some back.'

People stopped in their tracks and nodded. At least it was a positive suggestion.

'We could do that.' The Chief Elder was relieved. He consulted with his colleagues, then with a stronger voice said, 'Yes, we have decided that three villagers will go to the Great City. They will take contributions from all of us and they will buy whatever will bring us greater peace of mind.' Then he added, 'Of course we do not know what form that peace might take.'

Three men volunteered immediately. Rarely did anyone go to the Great City. It would be a journey of a lifetime.

Each family was asked to contribute ten tigs towards the trip, and two days later the men said farewell to a crowd of well-wishers and led three of the most reliable pack donkeys towards the slope that would take them inland through the mountains towards the Great City.

As they climbed, the thin grass gave way to grey aromatic scrub, which flavoured the air with herbs.

At first the track led them up through the green olive groves and the perfume of the orange trees, then up through the grazings where the bells on the necks of the goats rang in the air. They waved to the goatherds. As they climbed, the thin grass gave way to grey aromatic scrub, which flavoured the air with herbs. There was little shade here and the sun shone hot. Higher up, most of the vegetation gave way to yellow rock that crunched and rolled under their feet.

They had three days of walking up and down. They could not take the most direct route as they had to visit sources of water; the wayside wells, springs and the large lake in the Middle Land. By night they lit a fire and told stories before rolling into their blankets under shelters made from odd bits of sail.

After two days the men were struggling. They had taken sticks to aid their walking but each footstep hurt. It was therefore a great relief, after a stop in the heat of the day, to round a bend and see the spires of the Great City piercing the purple haze and catching gleams of sun.

By the evening they were outside the decorated gates. Only now they were here did they talk of what they sought. What form was this peace of mind to take? A wise man or woman? But how could they persuade such a person to come with them? Their bag of tigs was a paltry reward. Could it be a book or written prayers or something else? They decided to set off in separate directions and ask whoever might know. They would meet by night at their shelter and share their stories. And so the next day they found a cool place beneath the walls for the donkeys and set out. One decided to go to the souk and talk to the traders, who tended to know the news from far and wide. Another walked among the great pillars that held up the library. Wise and learned people were often sitting contemplating in these places of shade. The third man found his way into the church with the highest spire and climbed the spiral staircase to the top thinking that there he must be in the nearest place to peace and wisdom. They met that night but none of them felt he had found what they sought. A little frustration grew. They had to come back with something. It was worse the following night when still they had nothing.

However, by now word was spreading among the people of the Great City that there were three men from the country seeking to purchase peace of mind. It took little time for a rogue to select suitably formal clothes and present himself to the villager who wandered among the pillars.

'So I understand, sir, that you are a seeker of a state of peace of mind,' he bowed slightly. 'Sir, I may be able to help you.'

'Yes, yes please,' the villager nodded.

'Sir, if I may ask you to come back here tomorrow with your companions, I will have something for you. Oh, and bring the money. I will give you very cheap peace of mind.'

The rogue then clicked his feet together, ducked his head again and went home. He found a small wooden box and three soft leather bags. Inside each bag, he put one of three round pebbles. He padded the bags in the box with scraps of silk and closed the box. He took paints, tassels and ribbons, decorated the box and tied it up with silk cord.

Delighted to be the one to succeed in their task, the villager rushed back through the pillars to his colleagues outside the gate and the next day all of them, feeling considerably relieved, went to the area outside the library. After a while the rogue turned up carrying the brightly coloured box.

'Your peace of mind, sir,' he said, 'in this box.' He held forward the box. But as soon as one of the men reached out to take it, he withdrew it. 'The money, my friends, the money.'

'So how does the peace of mind work?'

The rogue stood forward. 'So I will tell you. The contents of this box, when mixed with the essence from a human hand, automatically generate peace and wisdom,' he said. And then as an afterthought: 'Of course, my friends, the box must not be opened until it is in the safe hands of your elders.'

The three looked at each other and tentatively handed over the bag of money. The box looked important. Besides, they had been away for a while and each was getting a little homesick.

The next day the three bought food for the donkeys and themselves and set out, the precious box safely in the pack of the leading donkey. They were excited.

It was the third night of travelling. The next day they would be home. It was a dark night. The moon had shone earlier and was now hidden behind thick cloud. They were camped amongst the stones of a ruined temple. Before he slept, each man had been privately musing on how clever they had been, how they would be thanked for solving the problems of the village by so generously sacrificing their time and effort.

Then one man woke. As he lay there, he thought that maybe it would be only fair if he took a bit of the peace of mind for himself as his personal reward for such sacrifice. He quietly got up and felt his way around the walls to where the donkey packs were hooped over a higher chunk of ruin. He felt for the box and the cord that was tied around it and tentatively opened it. He felt inside. He felt three round objects, each encased in soft leather – good. No one would notice if one was missing. He pulled one out and stuffed it into his pocket, then carefully tied up the box, pushed it far down into the pack, and crept back to his blanket, his gown unfortunately sweeping over one of the others.

'Oh, you, Maruk. What you doing?' the man mumbled.

'Sorry, Tomas, drank too much last night,' said Maruk as he lay and pulled up the blanket, falling quickly into a satisfied sleep.

Tomas did not go back to sleep but lay there with similar thoughts to those of Maruk. After all these hardships, surely he deserved a bit of the prize. And he too crept to the donkey packs, felt for the box and drew out one of the two round objects in its bag. It felt quite like a stone – but if so, it was clearly invested in powers. He weighted the box in his hand. It did not feel too different. No one would notice that one had gone. He stuffed the bag into his pocket and returned to his blanket, managing, in the total blackness of the night, to trip over the foot of the third man, who grunted.

'Votky, so sorry,' said Tomas, 'just stretching my legs – cramp, you know.' Tomas rapidly found his blanket, checked the contents of his pocket and closed his eyes.

And Votky made a deserving case for himself too and stole across the dark ground to the donkey packs. He felt for the box; it seemed that it might have been heavier when they had first been given it, but that must be imagination. He undid it and felt inside. There was a hard thing in amongst the softness of the leather and he pulled it out in its bag and put it into his pocket. But now the box felt distinctly lighter. He must put something in to make up for the thing he had taken. He could see that dawn was just beginning to tint the edge of the sky. In panic he felt down on the ground for a pebble. Nothing. He felt around and touched something solid, not heavy, but rounded. He put it deep into the soft leather, closed the box, tied the silks and went back to his blanket, leaving a rather large, sleepy cockroach exploring the folds of leather inside the box in which it was now enclosed.

News passed round the villagers of Carasov that the men and donkeys had been sighted on the high mountain track and people gathered to make a welcoming party. They accompanied the men to the large communal hut where the elders waited to celebrate whatever had been brought back from the Great City. Once the hut was full of excited villagers, the doors were closed, as was customary. The Chief Elder stood lit by the only light source, which was a port in the thatched roof. All else was dark. His silk gowns of office flowed down over the small platform on which he stood. The box was ceremonially handed over. As the Chief Elder lifted the lid, something came out and ran straight into the fabric of his long sleeve, then the cockroach ran down the inside of the gown to the ground, in and out between feet on the earth floor until it reached the slit under the door and freedom. Meanwhile, faintly aware that something might have come out, the Elder felt inside the box for whatever else might be there. There was nothing more.

Finally he said quietly, 'Something fell from the box.'

In the dark and sweaty hut, the people crushed together as they were, bent down and felt around on the floor. But in vain. Finally they gave up. Gravely the Elder bowed his head.

'With deep regret I have to say that whatever it was that you brought back from the Great City has been lost.'

There was a great sigh. Yet another thing had gone wrong. People began to turn towards the door when a voice called out.

'Stop, my friends. Whatever it was that was brought back is still in here. The door was closed. Maybe if we want peace of mind, we just need to sit in here.' It was the young girl speaking, she who had suggested going to the Great City.

And that is what happened. After that day, whenever any villager in Carasov felt the need for some peace of mind, she or he would sit in the communal hut in the dark for a while, and invariably would feel a sense of profound peace. And things became better in Carasov. People were nicer to each other again and celebrated the arrival of spring with a joyous feast. And, for better or worse, some say that later the communal hut was taken over and rebuilt as a first small church in the village.

A Coffin Stone for the Moon

I have been telling the story of 'The Buried Moon' for a long time. It is a story that fits Halloween, but it is too good just to restrict to one or two weeks a year. Here I have renamed it and simplified it a little. It is a story that folklorist Joseph Jacobs included in his collection More English Fairy Tales *(1893). Jacob had obtained the story from another collector, M. Balfour, who in turn had obtained it from local people when she travelled in north Lincolnshire. It is a story based in the Carrs, an area of bogland in the Ancholme Valley (Balfour, M. 1891).*

There was a time when parts of Lincolnshire were extensive bog, with little villages perched on areas of higher ground. The land is now good farmland but somewhere out on that farmland might be a large oblong stone that played a part in a strange and dark story.

The bogs of Lincolnshire were places of fear but people had to make a living and so they dug the soft peat out of the ground, selling it to others in the towns so they could make fires to warm their houses. However, the villagers only ever went out onto the bogs during daylight hours when they could see the safe tracks and paths between the bubbling muds, the deep reed beds and the pools of stagnant and stinking water. There were dreadful Things that lived in the bogs and the Things hated the men who dug the peat. They also hated daylight and the Moon for the light she shed at night. During times of light, they stole away in the reeds and in the stagnant pools, and it was during the darkness that they crept out, setting up a moaning and crying sound that hurt the air.

The Things were things of all sorts. There were boglins with black teeth, groping hands that seemed to belong to no one.

There were things not quite dead, skulls with glowing eye sock-
ets that rolled around. They popped up in the stagnant waters,
cut through the night with a stare and sank back into the foul-
ness. There were skeletons and will-o'-the-wykes with their rush
lanterns. Zipping through the air were cats driving broomsticks
and flying witches with black fingernails and hair that splayed out
behind them. Above the moaning and crying, there were shrieks
and howls. Like the local people, you would never want to be
there on a ark night. Never.

The Moon was always interested in what went on below her.
She would look down on the ways of the people and things of
the Earth. Although she could see nothing of what happened
on the Lincolnshire boglands because nothing happened when
she shone, she could hear the sounds. She decided to go down
and learn more.

So, having shone for a few hours, the Moon pulled clouds over
the sky, put on her largest black cloak, pulled up the hood, laced
on her black shoes and came down to the boglands. The moans
and terrible shrieks reached her before she touched the land. The
Things knew she was there and they raged in their hate for her
in the pitch blackness. The Moon knew the tracks and causeways,
having looked down on them for all time and as long as she kept
to the middle, she was safe from the groping hands and half death
things that grasped out at her from the slime. She ducked the
broomsticks and the pieces of spikey gorse with which the witches
tried to swipe her as they swung by. She avoided the muddy skulls
that rolled this way and that in the quaking mud and she held her
nose against the stench of the foul and stirred-up slime.

All was well until the Moon's cloak caught on a large branch
of gorse bush thrown down by the witches and she tripped
on her hem. She fell headlong on the track and immediately
struggled to rise. Now, above the moaning, the shrieks and cries

rose in celebration of her demise. The groping hands groped up onto the track, cats pawed and clawed and the dead Things grabbed at the fabric of the cloak. She felt the black nails of a witch scratching the gloves from her hands and tying her hands fast onto the bush.

The struggle went on. But suddenly, cutting across the cacophony there was a different kind of cry. It was that of a man who had been visiting friends in one of the bogside villages. He had become lost on his way home in the terrible darkness and he had slipped off one of the stone bridges over the stagnant pools. He was desperately calling on the will-o'-the-wykes to use their light to show him back onto the track but they flew away. Wanting to help the man, the Moon struggled harder

The Moon struggled harder than ever and the hood of her cloak slipped back and suddenly there was the brilliance of pale yellow light over all the bogs.

than ever and the hood of her cloak slipped back and suddenly there was the brilliance of pale yellow light over all the bogs. Everywhere Things scrambled and slid, slipped and stumbled back into the slime. Now able to see the track, the man hauled himself from the bog and ran as fast as he had ever run, making for the nearest group of cottages.

The Moon was still caught. The gorse bush ripped at her cloak and a will-o'-the-wyke, with great effort, pulled her hood up again and thus extinguished the moonlight. The struggle continued for hours of the long night. The Moon was getting tired and the Things whooped with greater joy at winning the battle with their enemy. But now a faint streak of light appeared in the eastern sky – the beginning of dawn – the beginnings of daylight. The Things had to return to their horrible homes.

There was a quick conversation between the witches, jabbing at each other with their fingernails. For a moment other Things disappeared – then reappeared, hundreds of them, carrying on their backs one of the great stone slabs from the nearest bridge. The Things gathered round the stone, lifted one end and with huge effort and an even louder cry, they pushed the stone down on the Moon, burying her. Then with a variety of plops, plunges and bubblings, they disappeared and there was quiet. An innocent mist rose from the bog and in the gathering light, snags of the Moon's cloak fluttered from the gorse bush in a dawn breeze. A single will-o'-the-wyke was left on guard under the bush with his pinpoint of light.

The people of the villages knew nothing of the events of that night. They went about their chores of tidying the peat that had been dug that day, feeding their pigs and hens and stirring the pottage for their meals. Night drew on and a woman, who risked peeping her head from her door at night, noticed that it was even darker than usual.

'Coal black night, that is,' she said.

Then others noticed how the dark nights went on.

'Time the Moon was shining,' they said.

And because it was dark, the moans and shrieks of the Things were getting louder and the Things were getting bolder, creeping towards the edges of the bog, creeping towards the villages. After a week or two of the dark nights, Sam Taylor heard a crying Thing outside his cottage. Old Jenny's shutters were deliberately rattled and the thatch on Jake the wheelwright's roof was parted and an eye was staring in. People barred their doors and shutters and kept fires going all night inside the cottages and they did not sleep as the moaning grew night after night.

'Something strange is up. Not normal,' said Jake. The people put straws in their hats and new pennies into their pockets, hoping this would keep them safe but the great darkness continued. Finally a group of men decided to take a trip to see the Wise Woman Jayne who lived on the other side of the boglands. They set out early so as to be back well before dark.

'Yes, I had heard. Come inside,' said Wise Jayne.

They entered. Wise Jayne lived in a hut by Seacombe Rise. The men told her of the darkness and the encroachment of the Things of the bog. She nodded, and her sharp eyes watched them from behind a curtain of grey hair as they spoke. Then she disappeared into the back of the hut and reappeared with a large and ancient book. Her old fingers moved from symbol to symbol on the parchment.

'I need to know more,' she said, 'but for now here is a keep-safe to ward the Things from the cottages. Each villager should sprinkle salt on his door sill and hang a button and straw from the latch.'

The keepsafes helped a little but still the moanings, the shrieks and cries were there and people sensed Things moving on the tracks between the cottages. Still there was no Moon. A few brave souls visited the village to see if they could help and it was while yet another visitor was being told the story in the village inn that something happened. A man over the other side of the room overheard the talk. He was staying overnight there and came over.

'I'm just thinking – I just might be able to help you,' he said. ''Twas back some weeks on another visit here. I was lost on the bog tracks. It got dark. I fell into the bog. I was being dragged down by the Things. Dreadful it was.' He put his hands to his face for a moment, remembering, and then told them how suddenly the light of the Moon glowed out from somewhere on the bogs and he was able to find his way out of the mud and off the bogland. 'The Moon,' he said. 'She may be in our bogs, not in the sky.'

The next day the men went back to Wise Jayne with the news. She nodded and brought out her book again.

'You be brave men,' she said, looking them in the eyes. 'Go out tonight onto the bogs. Take forked hazel twigs and use the sticks to find for you a large oblong stone. It is the coffin stone of the Moon. It is lit by a single lantern and on the bush there is a sign of a star. Lift the stone.'

The men looked at each other in horror at their task.

Jayne went on. 'And speak not a word. To this end, put large stones in your mouths.'

The men walked home reflecting on the night to come. They did not tell their families what was to happen but silently left their cottages two hours after dark and met. They carried crooks with which to feel the way. The moaning and sighing seemed louder than ever that night. They put the stones into their mouths and walked out on the track to the bog. For hours they searched. They were bullied and taunted by groping hands, tripped by the rolling skulls. Witches thrashed them with gorse, cats squealed in their ears, but finally one man saw a strange star shape on a bush; it was a piece of fabric caught on prickles. There was a single light there too and tapping on the ground. The man felt the cold strike of stone. He signed to the others and they used their crooks to lever up the stone. The great stone gradually rose.

Suddenly there was a huge pale circle of yellow light from the ground. It lit all of the bog. The smiling face of the Moon stared up at the men. Instantaneously there was a great cry that split the air, then cries, bubblings and ploppings then silence. And the Moon was shining down on them from high up in the sky.

The Moon has never forgotten how the men of the Lincoln village saved her from the dreadful grave in the boglands. And as I say, somewhere on the farmlands is a great stone …

The Splattering of Magic

When I am walking, I often pick up a stone. There is something comforting about having a stone in my hand. Some stones come home with me and then I am not sure what to do with them so there are various piles of rocks in my house and garden. That could, of course, pose problems to a future geologist or archaeologist who might care to wonder as to how all these different stones can have come together – but that is another story. Sometimes as I carry a stone, I anthropomorphise. I think of the experiences through which that stone has existed. I wonder where it has been, how it came to look like it does, what it has seen. If it is half a stone, where is the other half? The writing of this story came from the sort of imagining that follows such thought. As a number of the stories in this book suggest, stones can have amazing histories. The stone in the story below is no exception.

The stone in this story is an evenly round stone (it has to roll). For me there is something specially comforting about a round stone to roll in my hand. When I tell this story I often take with me such a stone and pass it through the audience. Finding round stones is not easy. Stones are shaped by the form of erosion that they have encountered, waves, stream, river or wind, rock or sand. There are only a few places where I have seen such roundness – one is on the beaches of South Glamorgan in Wales, where there are broad flat layers of stone with gullies. Rolling and crashing around in the gullies seems to create the rounded form.

This is a story about how Sam came to have amazing powers for just one hour of his life – and how he could have become very rich indeed, but he did not and that was all right.

Long ago, far back from the current time, there were wise women who helped the people of the world to be sensible and to sort out the trials and tribulations of life. The wise women then lived in the far corners of the world, in caves beside spectacular wells. Most ordinary people never saw them. The wise women managed the flow of good works through the world mostly through the people that they trained to be wizards, sages, sorcerers and shamen, but the real power was with the wise women. They worked with a form of power that sadly, we rarely see today.

Once the sorcerers and their like had a basic training, they went out into the world and set themselves up on the edges of villages and helped the villagers to manage everyday problems. As the sorcerers acquired experience of, for example, calling in rain clouds, or getting apples to ripen more quickly, or helping people to sort out arguments, they moved on to larger places and bigger tasks. It took them at least three lifetimes to become proper sorcerers.

Mogum was a very junior sorcerer who lived outside the little village of Ug. He had had a very basic training and he had set himself up in a cave under the cliffs by a stream. The stream ran near the circle of huts and stalls under the trees where the villagers lived. Because he was only in his first lifetime as a sorcerer, Mogum only did small spells – but he tried hard and generally the villagers were quite pleased with him. Every day, folks would wander up the wooded paths from the village, over the rickety footbridge to Mogum's cave to ask him to cast spells for them. They might ask him to keep the pigeons from the kale in their vegetable patches, for example. Mogum would then go inside his cave and consult the slates on which he had scribbled the formulae for spells that seemed about right and he would grind and mix, stir and blend, wet and dry the contents of jars and pots in order to make the potions and lotions that made his spells. Did they work? Well – sometimes they worked and if they did not work, the villagers would usually persuade themselves and their friends that they had worked – that there were fewer pecked leaves for a day or two. For his trouble, the village folk would give Mogum bread and pieces of cheese or perhaps some apples from the orchard, or a new baked scone. People would not ask Mogum for big spells because they knew that he was not yet ready. This was almost an unspoken rule.

But one day, a cheeky little lad broke the rule.

'Mr Mogum,' he said. 'Mr Sorcerer, I want you to give me magic powers for an hour.' His friends were watching him from the other side of the bridge and they giggled. It was a dare.

Mogum slowly shook his head. 'Too advanced for me,' he said gravely. But as the boy ran off, Mogum thought. Mogum was as clever as most sorcerers at this stage of their development, but he was also foolish. He thought, 'If I can give this cheeky boy the power he wants, perhaps I can jump a lifetime and get to being a real sorcerer more quickly. How impressed all my classmate sorcerers would be. How pleased with me our wise woman would be.'

He grunted agreement with himself and called the boy back and told him to return in three days. Then he went to the back of his cave where he kept his slates, looked at the scribbles and scratches for promising formulae and started to reach to the rocky shelves where there were rows and rows of corked stone jars with herbs and spices, crystals and powders and all the other substances from which he made his lotions and potions. That is, at least, how one shelf was. The other nineteen were higgledy-piggledy and anything but orderly. Mogum had not yet learned to be a tidy sorcerer. He lifted down several jars and shook their contents into a large bowl. He reached to another shelf for a mortar and pestle, a larger bowl and a pounder, a crusher and a musher. He took down a sieve and ladle and a spurtle that hung from a line strung across two stalactites. Now, he hoped, he had most of what he needed to make his mixture.

The last thing was a trip into the forest for the special toadstool that was going to be key to the spell. He found one under the great beech tree. The fungus was bright yellow with purple spots. Carefully Mogum carried it back to his cave. Then he remembered he also needed a red caterpillar and he huffed and puffed through the undergrowth all the rest of the day until he found one.

Now he set to and variously mushed and crushed, mixed and stirred, cooked and cooled. Then he waited for the mixture to mature. It was three days before Mogum thought he might have the right stuff to cast the spell that could give the boy special powers for an hour. He dusted down his most impressive gown and called the boy back. The brown mixture was now in a cauldron that hung over a fire outside the cave. As the boy came over the bridge with a nervous smile on his face, Mogum started chanting. He walked around the fire, every so often stirring the mix with the great wooden spurtle. Flames licked the cauldron. The brown mix bubbled and danced. It looked like gravy, though with each stir, it seemed to be turning more blue. Mogum beckoned the boy forward and gave him the spurtle.

'Now stir hard,' he said.

The blue gravy became suddenly more animated. Bubbles grew larger. Red streaks appeared. The boy backed off and rather rapidly Mogum took over again. Then there were sparks flying out into the air.

'Good, good,' Mogum said. 'Good, good …', trying to reassure himself. The boy was now nearly back at the bridge. There were flashes and bangs now, and all the other things were happening that happen when a spell goes seriously wrong. Then the stuff was bubbling over down the cauldron into the fire. As it touched flames, an enormous deep rumble growled up the valley. A flash of lightning seared from the cloudless sky and everything was obscured in thick blue smoke.

Then there was the explosion. The stuff splattered everywhere. It was all over the place. The boy had escaped and was back in the village, safe and assuring everyone that he had nothing at all to do with it. Mogum, shaking with shock, looked down at his gown. It was more like cobweb than fabric. He looked at his cave. It was a mass of fallen rock and rubble. The roof had collapsed and liquids and substances were running across the ground in every direction from broken jars.

'Oh dear, oh dear,' said Mogum. Then, as any other self-respecting sorcerer would have done, he wandered off to look for a new village and a new cave where the people had not heard of his mistake.

The stuff splattered everywhere.

As I said, all this happened a very long time ago. As time passed through the centuries, the ground by the cave on which Mogum's mixture had splattered was covered in dust and earth. Plants seeded there and people noticed that these grew strangely large. Leaves were three times as big as usual, flowers were huge and fruit that grew there was exceptionally juicy. People visited the place to see the plants, and storytellers nearby told the story of Mogum and his big mistake and then made up some other stories about Mogum that were not true. Parents told these to their children as they lulled them to sleep.

Then one year there was a disastrous flood. The giant trees fell and were swept away and now a river ran through the place. The pieces of rock broken in the explosion became rounded and rolled in the river waters down to the sea and settled on the beach and it was only the stories that remained. The plants were forgotten.

One day, in the time of Queen Victoria, a girl was walking on the beach. Her parents like many others of the time had just discovered the joy of visits to the seaside. The girl picked up a pebble. It was particularly round and smooth. She held it in her hand. While she may well have been told the story of Mogum the Giant – for that was now the story that was told – she had no idea that the pebble that she held had been part of Mogum's cave, and had been splattered with his mixture. The girl's father caught up with her and reached for her hand.

'What's this Abigail, a lovely round stone?' he said. 'Put it in your pocket and you can play with it at home.' She put it into her pocket and forgot it was there and when the maid came to do the laundry, she found the stone and threw it into the kitchen garden. It landed under a scented rose bush.

As happens in modern times, the Victorian houses were demolished. The ground was flattened, tracks were built then made into hard roads, then the builders came in and houses went up. Sam's house was built there and his family moved in. Sam liked to build things and he wanted to dig holes in the new garden but his parents were beginning to create a smooth lawn and pretty garden beds, so Sam's dad made him a sandpit.

On a day in early autumn the sun was shining a lovely gold. The sandpit had just been filled with new yellow sand. Sam raced down to the sandpit as soon as he could after school. It was under an apple tree and sometimes a small apple would drop into the sand. That gave Sam an idea. He built up a large sandcastle and, with his spade, created a spiral track from the top to the bottom. He collected up several of the apples and tried running them down the track. The first one ran halfway down before rolling off, but then the rest of the apples rolled off the track near the top. They were not sufficiently round, so Sam looked about for something else. In one of the new garden beds, he picked up an unusually round pebble. It felt nice and comfortable in his hand, just as it had felt for the Victorian girl, but of course, Sam knew nothing of its history. He was just about to roll it down the track on his sandcastle, when he heard his mother calling him for tea. He was hungry and she had said it would be his favourite meal, sausages and chips. He ran in, at first holding the round stone and then slipping it into his pocket.

The hour that followed was one such as Sam and his mum and dad had never known before and have never known since.

Sam reached the back door and sat on the step, pulling his sandy trainers off and anticipating the juicy sausages. 'I can't smell chips,' he thought, persuading himself that the smell had yet to reach him.

'Mum, it is chips isn't it? '

'No, love, I'm sorry but I decided that as Dad is out tomorrow, we had better finish the joint tonight – so it's cold meat and salad. I've got those nice little tomatoes that you like …'

'But you said it was sausage and chips and I wanted sausage and chips,' said Sam. 'I wish we could have sausage and chips. You promised.' Sam had his fingers in his pocket, rubbing the round stone to comfort his disappointment.

And then … well. When dogs smell something good, their noses twitch and this is exactly how it was with Sam and his mother because they could suddenly smell the most delicious smell of sausage and chips. It filled the kitchen. They looked around in surprise, and there on the table, in one of Mum's best dishes, were steaming, golden, crispy chips and on one of her flowery flat plates were brown sausages. Sam reached forward and took a chip and it was as good as it looked.

'Oh Mum,' he said, 'you were teasing.' Looking at his mum, he expected a smile, but he thought she looked a little white and she didn't smile. 'You all right, Mum?'

She was about to say that something very weird was happening when Sam's father walked in.

'What's this smell of chips? Thought it was cold meat and salad tonight.' Sam's mother tried to explain to him that she had not cooked the chips or the sausages and that they had arrived as a complete surprise, but he did not believe her and in the end she stopped trying to persuade him.

'Better get on with it then,' she said, and they sat down and had the delicious meal that was in front of them. And not only that but when Sam wished for ketchup, it was there. When he wished for coleslaw, that too came, but his fingers were on the stone in his pocket.

They started to talk about what had happened.

'It's because I wished,' said Sam.

'You don't just wish for something and it happens,' said Dad. 'Now look. I think I'll wish for a piece of best fillet steak, and of course it won't happen.'

Of course it didn't happen.

'Wish I could have some mayo,' said Sam. He was holding his knife and fork in his hands. Mum got up and fetched the mayonnaise from the cupboard, but not in a magical way at all.

They finished the sausages and chips. Sam sat back, still thinking about wishing. He put his hand in his pocket, again touching the stone.

'I know,' he said. 'I wish … I wish we could have creamy ice cream with chocolate sauce, some chocolate cake, the fizzy drink we had on holiday.' He reeled off a list. By the time he had finished, the table was groaning with the weight of the sweet wonders on his wish-list.

'Well … ' said his father.

'Well … ' said his mother. 'I wish I knew what was going on.' But of course, she did not have the stone, so her wish did not come true. 'I think we should eat the ice cream before it melts.'

Sam, his mother and father set out on eating again. They were very confused and it was a relief to do something familiar like eat – and eat – and eat.

'We'll think about it later,' said Sam's father. He was shuffling towards the most comfortable chair with his hand on his middle.

Though Sam and his parents did not know it, by the time they had sat back, the hour of magic power had run out. The stone, that had so long ago been splattered by the magic of Mogum's spell potion was no longer any more than a comfortable, round stone that was working its way towards the hole in the corner of Sam's pocket.

Sam and his mother and father never did know that they could have used the magic for anything in the world, but they were a happy family and so maybe that was just as well.

The Rainbow Stones

As I write this, it has become the 'thing' to draw or paint designs on stones and leave them in specific or special places. Some have words on them too. There is a sense that if the stone means something to you, you can take it. This process developed into an interesting mystery in the Devon village in which I live. A couple of years ago someone took time and care in painting stones and placing them outside the doors of specific houses and cottages. No one knew who did it. He or she was never seen. Every so often another stone would be added. Rumours circulated. I was not the culprit but felt mildly honoured when I was asked, 'Is the stone painter you?'

Added to the painted stones, the story also draws on a fascination that I had, or have, with the idea that there are small other worlds hidden in deep grass, by rock pools or springs; other people who have a different world from humans.

The story draws on plenty of other folk story inspirations, 'the stuff' of folk tales.

Juliana shifted the grey stone from hand to hand. It was smallish, roundish and fairly ordinary as stones go. Her family sat with her by a fire that danced in her old fireplace. Brass fire tools glinted in comfort.

'Special,' she said. 'Precious. Feel it.' She handed it to Peter.

'You going to tell us a story then?' Kerry twisted her finger in her hair. It felt like this was the way best of Juliana's stories started.

'Yes,' Juliana paused. 'You know some stories are true and some are less true. You must keep this stone safe because this story is more true.'

Mouths opened to ask questions but Juliana persisted.

'It was a Sunday,' she said. 'On Sundays the family went for a walk – every Sunday. Not that everyone wanted to go especially when it was raining like it rained that day. But it was what they did. Through the wood, through the village and back past the church. Getting "a bit of fresh air", as mother said. Doing homework was the alternative and putting that off was always a good idea.'

Juliana was gazing at the flame.

'It was that day when … ' she hesitated, apparently thinking of a name, 'when Jay found the first rainbow stone. She had wandered ahead, scuffling feet in the autumn leaves and worrying about school on Monday. And as leaves fluttered up at the foot of a tree, there it was, like a jewel, a smooth round pebble; one that had rolled in a stream for hundreds of centuries, but it was painted with an extreme beauty of touch. Fine lines of different but brilliant colour covered every surface, like rainbows in oily water or exquisite weavings or tapestries.'

Juliana spoke in a dreamy voice.

'Everyone looked at the stone and admired it and decided they should leave it there. Maybe it was waiting for someone.'

'That stone?' asked Peter.

'Not this one, but one like it. Listen to the story.

'The family went home and then there was the usual stress and shouting about homework. Jay found school work very hard. She hated school and those who might have been her friends thought she was stupid, so she was lonely too. No one knew it then, but she was clever. She thought and imagined a lot.

'Soon after that there was a day when Jay felt particularly cross and upset and she decided to go off into the woods. She wasn't allowed to go alone but she went. She clicked the latch on the garden gate and walked the path to the wood. She needed something special after another horrible day at school made worse by her sister bragging about another achievement badge. Jay went down into the dell. There was a clearing there where lush grasses and reeds had rooted in soggy earth. Beyond were the crags of a cliff. She pushed through the grasses towards the cliff. She had only been here once before with friends and then they had not noticed the spring hidden in the rocks. The water bubbled and rippled. Birds sung. It was a special place. Jay bent to sip the water, feeling it might clear her mind. Then she sensed movement. A small face was peering from a hole in the rock. Jay's heart leapt. Had she really seen something? Then three men were there. Pixies. They had to be pixies – what else? They were wiry and everything about them seemed to be brown except for gingery hair that stuck out like her brother's. Jay stared and they stared at her before slowly pulling back behind the rock. She waited but they did not return. Then it was time to go home and once she had climbed out of the dell it seemed more and more likely that she had been dreaming.

'Jay came back to the dell the next day. She had to find out. She brought some raisins and crouched where she had been the day before. Could it happen again?

'The pixie people appeared again and she held out three raisins. Each nodded his head and took a raisin, eating it slowly, bright eyes peering at her over the raisins, which to them were the size of apples. She tried talking quietly to them. In response they muttered sounds like the chattering of birds on a still day. They disappeared and came back with beech nuts, which they held out to her.

'She came back to the dell whenever she could get away unseen. She was still unsure if what was happening was some sort of dream. Over the next few days the ritual exchange of gifts occurred. Mostly Jay recognised what she was given but not the little hard brown balls. When she looked curious, one of the pixies ate one in front of her. She risked it, crunched one and a strong garlic taste filled her mouth, rose up to her nose and nearly made her sneeze. At tea, Jay's mother noticed the garlic smell.

'"Picking the wild garlic then. Good for you, but the smell's not so good for us!" she laughed and her brother pinched his nose. So, Jay thought, if they can smell the garlic, the meetings with the pixies are not dreams.

'The next time Jay went to the spring, three pixies appeared. They held a stone, like the rainbow stone she had found, but this time the bright colours were fine threads woven over the surface of the stone. As she was admiring it, turning the stone over in her hands, a girl pixie shyly appeared from behind the rocks. She was the same size as the men. She reached for Jay's hand and with her little hand, pulled Jay's finger, indicating that she should follow them. Jay followed along a tiny rocky path, through a gap in the bushes, and out into another clearing. Brambles and twigs caught on her T-shirt and she pulled herself clear. She was led towards an overhanging rock. In the black shadows underneath it, Jay could see a squirming mass of movement with hairy black sticks protruding and pulling back. One of the men disappeared into the blackness and a moment later led a large spider into the daylight. The lead was tied round the spider's abdomen. Jay had never feared spiders, though this one was large, and huge beside the pixie. The pixie stroked the spider's abdomen, and then began to lead it along the surface of a flat rock. As they walked, a strand of white silk came out of the spider's abdomen. A smaller pixie ran behind the spider, carefully winding the cobweb strand into a ball. Then the spider was led round and back under the ledge.

'Jay felt her hand being touched again. She was led now along the rocks to a small cave lit partly by daylight and partly by what looked like rush stems from which flared and flickered

A smaller pixie ran behind the spider, carefully winding the cobweb strand into a ball.

small flames. In a corner of the cave there were bundles of dried plants. Pixies in aprons were tying up bundles of the plants. As Jay got used to the light, she could see deeper into the cave where there were fires burning. Cauldrons hung over the fires and strands of coloured steam drifted up through a hole in the roof of the cave. In another part of the cave, balls of coloured cobweb were piled up. This cave must be where they dyed the cobweb strands. Pixies danced around her as she looked on with wonder. Then she was led to another cave into which she had to crawl. There were piles of round pebbles. Pixies sat at a loom weaving the coloured threads into fabric. Others were using some sort of glue to mould the fabric over the surfaces of the stones. And there was a pile of completed rainbow stones in amazing mixes of reds and blues, yellows and bright blues, turquoises and scarlets and emerald greens. Jay nodded in admiration and a pixie selected a small stone and gave it to her, closing her fingers round it.

'As Jay took the stone she thought she heard her mother's voice calling from far off. She signed a hurried farewell to the pixies and ran. As she shut the gate she was thinking of how she would show the stone to her mother but then she realised she would have to explain about going to the wood alone, and she decided to keep it as her secret.

'Over the next day or two, when she was struggling with her homework, Jay looked at the stone. It seemed to give her encouragement. It was different from the stone they had found. This one was covered by threads and the one they had found was apparently just painted.

'It was a few days before she could return to the dell. But this time, at first, there were no pixies. Then two appeared but without smiles or warm greetings. They gestured to her to follow and led her to the overhanging rock where the spiders had been kept. As they approached it, a flock of crows flew up, squawking. Pixies ran about shouting and waving their arms at the birds. The last bird flew up with a spider still wriggling in its beak and a tie flipping around its wings. It was evident what had happened.

'Jay went home, sad for her friends but at home there was commotion too. As Jay came through the back door, her sister was screaming and Mother was running from the kitchen with a glass tumbler and an old birthday card in hand.

'"Jay, where were you? We were looking for you. There's a big spider on your sister's desk and she's terrified. Would you move it for us?"

'Jay quietly put the tumbler over the spider and slid the card beneath. And as she did it an idea was forming.

"I want to study spiders. Where can I keep him?"

"Anywhere, but not in the house. The garden? Here." Mum pushed an empty margarine container into Jay's hand and hustled her towards the door.

"You – studying? Joke," her sister called out. She was always teasing and it hurt.

'Jay put leaves and sticks into the box, then the spider. She made holes in the lid and went off to look for more spiders. By the end of the morning she had a good collection. One or two of the spiders ate each other but then Jay found a source of dead flies on window ledges. She wished she had asked the pixies what they fed their spiders on. At lunchtime she showed her collection of spiders to her sister, who leapt up, screaming again. That was pleasing.'

Juliana had a strange and far-away smile on her face.

'Then Jay wanted to know more about spiders. Maybe not all of them would spin webs. She shut herself in her room with the family laptop and secretly brought the spider box in. At first she could not spell 'spider', but she worked it out. She struggled with reading words but very slowly now they started to work for her. Pictures were easier and she studied them in detail. Every so often she would open the box and look at the spiders, then go back to the screen. She found out which spiders made cobwebs and released those that did not. Vaguely aware of what was going on, her mother absolutely banned the box of spiders from the house. Jay waited until Mother was in her workroom then took the laptop out to the garage and continued.

'In the afternoon, Jay waited for the chance to go to the dell, then scooped up the box of spiders and ran. Three pixies came out looking bedraggled and unhappy but then Jay beckoned them to look in her box. Their chattering rose to a pitch when they saw all the spiders. A group of others appeared, gathering round the box then carrying it proudly on their shoulders to where their spiders had been kept. They looked to Jay. Carefully she opened the box again. And as each spider started to make a bid for freedom, it was grabbed and tied, then led to the space under the ledge. Other pixies brought bundles of what looked like dried flies and beetles and this was fed to the new spiders.

'The pixies bowed and smiled at Jay and placed another beautiful stone in her hand.

'Again Jay thought of showing the stone to her mother but when she got home, Mother was grumpy because the washing machine was out of order. And because mother was grumpy everyone else was grumpy. So again Jay kept the secret to herself. She had homework to do. Without being nagged this time, she reached for her reading book and took it to her room. She shut her door, set the stones beside her and it seemed that the words in the book came more easily than usual. When she had finished her reading, she borrowed the laptop to look up more on spiders.

'At school, her teacher noticed that Jay seemed to be trying harder, and her reading was suddenly improving. When they did a project on creepy crawlies the next week, it was Jay's hand that went up first each time to answer questions. At times she knew more than her teacher.

'"You like creepy crawlies, Jay?"

'Jay quietly nodded. "Especially spiders."

'School slowly became a different place for Jay. Reading was still hard, but it was now worth the struggle and the more she could read, the more she could find out about spiders and other creepy crawlies. The happier she was in school, the more she could do her reading and the more the other children wanted to play with her.

'Jay continued to visit the pixies, but less often now because she had friends to play with. The pixies greeted her each time she went, and sometimes she visited the spiders and watched them being walked along the ledge, with the cobweb rolled up behind them. Or she would watch the cobweb strands being dyed or the weaving. Sometimes she took new spiders to them. They showed her which spiders made the best silk for their work.

'Then there was the day of the party. Jay arrived in the dell to find pixies dancing round the spring to fine clear music that seemed to swim though her head and round and about the leaves on the trees. It came from a small group of pixies who played reed pipes. Others had drums. Their brown clothes were decorated with strips of woven cobweb in many colours. Jay watched and listened and they came up to her, and stroked her hand, smiling up at her.

'But it was the last time she saw the pixies. When she went back a few days later, they had gone. There was no sign that anyone had lived either by the spring or further along where the spiders had been kept. Autumn leaves were covering up the place where so much had happened. When she got home, Jay went straight to the corner of her wardrobe where she kept the two rainbow stones. They were there, but they now looked like the first stone the family had found. Threads were now fine lines of dye. The cobweb had dissolved, leaving the dyes. And over the years, the beautiful dyes faded too.'

Juliana fingered her stone again.

'This was one of the stones,' she said.

'J for Juliana? You were Jay?' Kerry questioned. Juliana smiled and, of course, they never knew.

2

ROCK AND
STONE IN USE

Rock and stone are cut from the earth by the stonecutters. They are the bowl for your soup, the salt with which you may season your soup and, according to one story, they make the soup itself. But then petrol is also a kind of prehistoric vegetable soup made over eons ...

Willow Pattern Story

This is the story of the design on Willow Pattern ceramic ware (known as Blue Willow in the USA). Ceramic ware includes porcelain and bone china. Porcelain is made from heating clays, including kaolinite, to above a thousand degrees centigrade. Bone china includes bone ash and feldspar (a common rock material) to give strength and translucency.

Willow Pattern ware was introduced in the UK in the late 1700s and this coincided with the shift from hand-painted ware to engraved and printed glaze transfers, which enabled much higher production levels. The initial inspiration for the design was Chinese hand-painted ware. The story below is not, however, Chinese in origin. A number of 'legends' were constructed for marketing purposes for the ware. One story, similar to that below, was published in a magazine, The Family Friend *as* The Story of the Common Willow Pattern Plate (Portanova, J. (no date but around the mid 1800s)). There are different versions of the story, possibly some earlier, and there are suggestions that it had political overtones concerning China and its internal and international relationships.

I have been telling the Willow Pattern story for some time. When I tell it, I take along some pieces of willow-patterned ware that depict the story. I find the material in an old town dump. Judging by the heavy nature and style of the ceramics, it dates from the mid-Victorian age. Where I find it, the pot is so abundant that it covers all the surface of the ground and a large proportion of it is willow pattern design.

The design on Willow Pattern ceramic ware.

Long ago in the east of China a rich and powerful and prob-ably dishonest Mandarin lived in a substantial house with wonderful landscaped gardens. A clear stream meandered through the gardens and the long tendrils of willows drifted and wavered in the passing waters. There was a pretty bridge and the Mandarin's daughter, Koong-See, spent much time sitting on a stone near to where the stream rippled under the bridge. She would spend her time sewing beautiful silk embroideries. She loved creating her pictures, but her father was very protective and she was isolated and lonely. She would watch the white doves come and go from the dovecot and wish that she was free like them.

Occasionally, however, she would meet Chang near the bridge. Chang was her father's bookkeeper and he was able sometimes to take a lunchtime walk. In their brief conversations, Chang and Koong-See developed warm feelings for one another. If the Mandarin ever caught them speaking, he would be angered. Chang was not of sufficient social status to be a suitor for his daughter and, for a while, the Mandarin would ensure that Chang had too much work to do to get out into the garden.

The Mandarin worked in the Customs service and this work entailed trips to the capital of the province. He usually took Chang with him, but one day there was a trip, a matter of deal-ing with bribes, that was somewhat too sensitive to risk Chang's presence. Now Chang was able to walk in the garden every day and he made sure that his route took him by the bridge. It was the time of the orange blossom and the petals fell gently as Chang and Koong-See fell in love. When the Mandarin returned, their feelings were too strong for the lovers to return to the pattern of occasional visits, and so they arranged secret trysts. The Mandarin found them. He was infuriated. Chang was immediately dismissed from his work and the Mandarin built a tall wall all around the garden and a tower by the stream's edge, in which he could incarcerate his daughter.

The Mandarin also decided that perhaps an even better way of keeping control over his daughter was immediately to find a 'suitable' husband for her. He asked around and found a nobleman, Ta-jin who was seeking a young wife. Ta-jin, as well as being older was unfortunately ugly – but he was wealthy. The betrothal was arranged and a wedding planned for the following spring. Only after all the planning was Koong-See taken to meet him. She was horrified at the idea of marriage to this man, but she could do nothing.

Hardly any contact between Koong-See and Chang was possible however hard they tried. But one day when Koong-See was allowed out of the tower for a short walk in the garden, she saw a little boat made out of a coconut shell floating down the stream. She caught it and inside was a note from Chang saying that whatever happened he would come for her and they would elope. She put a note into the coconut shell, assuring him of her love, and her wish that both of them could fly free from the cruelties – as free as the doves.

The day of the wedding neared. There was no word from Chang. Koong-See worried that he might have changed his mind. Then it was the wedding day. The wedding party gathered. Koong-See, looking deeply sad, but dressed in beautiful silk, carried a distaff as a symbol of virginity. Ta-jin carried a box of jewels as dowry. Suddenly one of the servants darted forward and grabbed Koong-See by the arm. It was Chang in disguise. He grabbed the box of jewels from Ta-jin, and ran with Koong-See over the bridge, chased closely by the wedding party, the Mandarin lashing the air with a fearsome whip.

The lovers got away and fled to the coast where, with the help of a boatman, they were able to reach an offshore island.

With the money from the jewels and from the silk wedding gown, they were able to buy the island and, happy at last, they set up house beside a beautiful willow tree.

However, Ta-jin and the Mandarin were not content to give in. An army of soldiers was amassed and an attack on the island was planned. Koong-See and Chang defended themselves as best they could, locking and barring the doors and windows, but when the soldiers set fire to the house, the combustible materials burned easily and the willow tree wilted and burned with a great crackling. As the smoke rose and the roof caved in, two white doves were seen to rise from the house and fly far away. The lovers were properly free at last.

Many elements in the story are represented in traditional Willow Pattern picture on ceramics. These include the Mandarin's house, the tower, the stream, bridge and willows, the orange trees. Crossing the bridge are Koong-See (holding a distaff or stick associated with spinning) and Chang (holding a box) followed by three figures, one carrying a whip. The boatman, island and the doves are also depicted.

The White Mountain

This is a tale about salt and it is rock salt as opposed to that produced by the evaporation of seawater. It is a retelling of a Russian folk tale, one of those collected by Arthur Ransome (of Swallows and Amazons *fame) in his years of living in Russia. His version was published in* Old Peter's Russian Tales *(Ransome, 1916), though the story is published elsewhere in various forms. It is a story that gives me a warm feeling. It is what I describe as 'rich' in that it displays colour, interesting experiences and some authenticity. It starts in a fairly conventional way with three brothers – but then it veers from many folk tale conventions. The youngest brother has been deemed to be a 'silly boy' – or as Ransome calls him, 'a ninny'. It is a tale that I think may be a combination of two stories. Just as one thinks one is coming to the happy ending, something happens and another very different narrative kicks in, albeit, briefly. That part I have modified slightly.*

There was a wealthy Russian merchant who owned many ships carrying cargoes far and wide across the seas. He had three sons who were of an age to begin to follow in his footsteps. He thought long and hard about how he would get them started as merchants. He talked with his wife. It was quite an easy decision for the two older sons as they had shown interest in his ships, the cargoes and the business of trading. He took them aside one day and told them that each would be given one of the new vessels that he had just had built, and as well, a good and trusted crew. On the ships to give them a start, there would be a full cargo of the best wines and vodkas, silver tableware and precious stones.

'Use what I have given to you wisely,' he said, 'and you will stand as successful merchants before long.'

With excitement, the two young men planned their journeys, met their crew and within a few days, had sailed off across blue waters.

The third boy, Ivan, waved goodbye to his brothers, wondering what his father had in mind for him. He knew he had not pleased his father. Instead of the sessions with tutors, he was in the woods, exploring, and instead of helping with the paperwork, he was away fishing. He liked to play the balalaika, sing and dance with his friends. His rather serious parents considered him a silly and rather worthless boy.

Ivan waited for his father to call him. Nothing happened. There was no new vessel being built and no valuable cargo being amassed, so maybe it would be something different. Eventually Ivan summoned courage and approached his father.

'What about me and my future, Father?'

'You?' said his father. 'You will make no merchant. You have no wisdom, no business skills and no determination. Why should I give you anything?'

Ivan could hardly hide tears. For days, he wandered around, pale and lost. Seeing the depth of his despondency, his mother put in a word for him to her husband.

'Give him a chance. That old ship you were going to scrap. Let him have that, some of the old men and some sort of cargo to play with.'

Angrily the father acquiesced. Ivan was given the ship. The cargo that arrived in donkey carts at the quay was sacks of scrap wood, metal pans and rags of clothing and canvas. And as Ivan was looking over it, a group of men arrived, some hobbling and two with sticks to help them to walk. He recognised several as men who had worked on his father's ships in previous years. This was his crew. At first Ivan felt as discarded as the rubbish in front of him, but then the sailors smiled and one said, 'Can't wait to feel the heaving deck beneath me.'

And from then on Ivan was determined to make his fortune and that of his men in the best way he could. They raised the grubby and torn sails in a fresh breeze and hauled up the anchor. The ship made slow progress but the crew settled, singing their old shanties as they heaved the ropes, and worked the tiller, and from their pockets they got out their sail repair kits. Meanwhile, Ivan scrubbed the decks and cleaned the cabin. There were two calm days but then the sky blackened, and the water ripples drew up into a swell, the wind howled and large waves crashed on the fragile vessel. There was the sound of ripping sailcloth and the rotten rudder gave way. They rigged a makeshift steering gear, but still the ship drifted. Then the weather calmed. Purple land was in sight and they managed to steer towards a gentle shore where, in warm shallow waters, the ship promptly sunk. The tide ebbed and the ship now lay, a sad mess, heeled over on the sand. There were no other people and no villages in sight.

When they had all recovered, Ivan announced that he would go ashore to see what he could see and he ordered the men to muster their skills and use anything from the cargo to repair the ship. Soon there was the singing of shanties as men sat patching and sewing sails, whipping and splicing rope and hammering calking into the planks. On the next tide, the ship floated again.

Ivan found a track and walked inland through windblown trees. Then there were low mountains, but they were strangely white. The sun shone bright on them and nothing grew. His clogs crunched. It could have been snow, but it was not cold. He bent and drew his finger across the white and touched his tongue. It was salt. Soon he came to tunnels and deep holes in the ground, salt mines but still no people. There was no one anywhere.

They managed to steer towards a gentle shore.

Salt was valuable. Ivan knew this. In seconds he was running back to the shore. His ship bobbed on the water, patched and seaworthy again, and with a newly cleaned hold. Soon he and the crew were filling sacks with salt from the salt mountains and carrying them back to the ship. It was grinding work for the old men.

Two days later, in warm sunshine and on a calm sea, with a full cargo of salt, the little ship sailed off from the island, now ready to do some proper trading. There followed three days of gentle sailing during which the sailors and Ivan were able to rest their strained backs and soothe their red raw hands.

Then another land was sighted. Buildings and towers reflected the sun. It was a land of some wealth and they made sail for a harbour. Fishermen, singing and talking as they mended their nets, were surprised to see the little ship with a patchwork of sails drifting in amongst their craft. Ivan tidied himself and asked directions to the house of the Tsar of that town and then he set off with a wooden box of salt to visit the Tsar.

'I have granted you audience,' said the Tsar, 'though I don't know you. So who are you and what have you come for?' Ivan bowed his head. The Tsar raised his hand showing off the quality of his silk cuffs.

'I, sir, am a merchant, bringing with me the fruit of the earth,' said Ivan, realising he was not sure how a wealthy merchant would present himself.

'You have brought something for me to see?' said the Tsar.

'Yes, it's salt. Taste it.' Ivan proffered the box. Before he had a chance to stop him, the Tsar had taken a very substantial pinch of salt and piled it onto his tongue.

'Ugh – no. Take your stuff and go.' He was shouting for servants as Ivan withdrew and as he hurried away, three servants raced towards the Tsar, carrying stone jars of water. Outside the house, in the shade of the walled garden, Ivan cursed himself. Maybe he was Ivan the Silly after all. He should have realised what would happen. A kitchen maid passed by and asked him what he was doing there.

'Just resting. Just thinking,' he said. 'And I'm thirsty.'

'Come, think in the kitchen and have a drink.'

Ivan settled in the corner of the kitchen and idly watched the busy cooking that was going on around him. The Tsar's meal was being prepared. Cooks and maids scurrying hither and thither, cutting up meat, chopping carrots, slicing cabbages, crying over onions. He was intrigued. 'But now, do they use salt?' he asked himself. He saw no salt. There were herbs and spices, mustard and sauces but no salt.

A bell tolled. It was time to serve the Tsar his dinner. Immediately all the kitchen staff repaired to the store to collect the serving platters. Ivan sprang into action. There were pots of stews, turnips, cabbage and rice. He sprinkled salt from his box in all the pots and gave the contents a quick stir. He was just sitting back in his chair when the cooks and maids returned, hands full of serving ware. The meal was served. The kitchen staff came and went and Ivan waited.

Then there was talk of how delighted the Tsar, the Tsarina and the Tsarevna, their daughter, were with today's tasty food. What was different? The Tsar asked to see the cooks. Four cooks straightened their aprons, adjusted their caps and went in to see him. They shook their heads and returned. Maybe the maids had done something different. Six serving maids went in and returned. They could think of nothing different either and the Tsar now asked to see anyone else in the kitchen. Someone remembered Ivan and he was sent in.

'You again? Did you have anything to do with the food in the kitchen?'

'Sir, I added a little pinch of salt to each of your dishes,' said Ivan, head bowed.

'That white stuff?' the Tsar paused. 'I want to buy some. I will buy all that you have.'

'Now,' thought Ivan. 'Now I must think as a real merchant.'

'The white stuff is worth much gold and silver.'

'Name your price,' said the Tsar.

A few days later the little ship had a cargo of gold and silver in place of the salt and the crew had sore backs again but they were happy. Ivan had had a particularly happy few days as the loading and unloading progressed. He had spent it with the Tsarevna. She was fascinated by this strange and resourceful young man. When the ship was loaded, she asked if she could see over it. With the full and somewhat valuable cargo, the ship was now anchored outside the harbour and Ivan proudly rowed her to it. She wanted to see everything. She asked about the sails and they were hoisted for her to see. She asked why the ship did not sail when the sails were up and she was shown the anchor chain.

'But I want to see the anchor itself,' she said.

Now this is the point in the story where Ivan may have gone back to being a silly boy, or on the other hand he may have been very devious – or hopelessly lovestruck. He asked his men to raise the anchor and promptly took the princess down below to see his cabin. She did not feel the ship shudder into motion. And by the time they had been served with tea and cakes, the ship was well away from land.

Seeing her country far away on the horizon, the Tsarevna cried for two hours, during which time Ivan did his best to comfort her. And then she decided that the comfort of Ivan was worth the sacrifice of her homeland. For the next week, the ship sailed without a lot of attention from Ivan who was otherwise occupied in ensuring the comfort of the Tsarevna.

Now they neared the Russian mainland coast. Ivan could not wait to show his father how well he had done, with the precious cargo, and a Tsarevna as a bride. But that night, when, arm in arm, the two were gazing at the stars, they saw two large white sails heading in the same direction as they.

'It must be my brothers,' said Ivan. 'Let's alter course to see how they've got on.'

The little ship altered course and made contact with the two ships, which were indeed those of Ivan's brothers. There were apparently warm welcomes and introductions, but when the two boys realised that their 'silly' brother had done so much better than them, they devised a plan. The next night, as Ivan did his late-night tour round his ship, they came at him from behind and threw him overboard.

In the morning, the story was that careless Ivan had fallen over the stern, probably following too much celebratory vodka.

The two brothers would split his possessions between them and sail immediately for home. The Tsarevna was devastated, especially when she was considered to be half of the possessions and was forcibly betrothed to one of the brothers. Her tears were unstoppable.

Ivan did not drown but swam for a while, then he found a large log and was able to scramble on to it. Within hours he found himself on a sandy beach. He lay exhausted for a while and awoke to look into two massive eyes in a massive face staring down at him. He blinked. It was real. He had landed on the fabled Island of Giants that every child had been told about, and which no one had ever seen.

The Giant was kind. He took Ivan to his house and sat him on a log next to a huge fire. He could see that Ivan was deeply troubled, despite his lucky escape from drowning.

'So what is it, little man?' the Giant's voice rumbled.

Ivan told his story.

'No problem,' said the Giant, picking up Ivan and placing him on his shoulder. 'We'll upset the wedding plans of that brother of yours and put things right.'

The Giant marched into the sea, waded through the waves and pushed his way through the deeper waters. So tall was the Giant that Ivan got no more than his toes wet. Then they were wading up on a beach that Ivan knew and within seconds they were outside the walls of Ivan's father's house. Ivan peeped over the walls from the Giant's shoulder. There was a great wedding going on inside, people eating, drinking and dancing to musicians. The groom was the elder of Ivan's brothers, and the bride was his Tsarevna, who was crying into a large handkerchief. A man in fine silk robes was moving towards them, evidently to seal the marriage.

Ivan was already slithering down the Giant's back, saying thank you, thank you as he landed and ran to the gate.

The Giant grinned, 'Say nothing about me. I like to remain a mystery, a giant fairy story.'

Ivan rushed in. People did not recognise him and tried to bar his way. In the kerfuffle everyone looked around. The Tsarevna looked up and she was the only one to recognise Ivan. She tore through the crowd, her gown flying behind her, calling his name and falling into his arms. The father stepped forward asking what was happening, demanding for this interloper to be caught.

It was not long before Ivan was recognised by everyone and the explanation was given, mainly by the Tsarevna. Ivan's wealth was restored to him and in a few days the Tsar and Tsarina had been collected from their island and a grand wedding was blessed by both families. The Merchant was all smiles, even when his two older sons declared that they would be away on business.

In the introduction to the story, I indicated that this feels like two stories or perhaps one that has been later extended. It is the section about the Giant that I consider separate from the longer initial section.

Two Happenings in the Lives of Beryl and Bill

The story below is modern. The first part was shared by a friend, Bill, at a story event in my house. I needed some humorous material for a concert and linked the first part with another bit of humour from somewhere. I will say a little more after the tale is told!

Beryl and Bill were a lovely couple, and indeed, they loved each other very much. They took care of their health and had already lived to a ripe old age. Each day they would drive up to the heathland that overlooked their village and take a walk there.

It was a morning in autumn. They had parked the car in the heathland car park and were setting out on their constitutional. They loved nature and admired the plants and insects as they walked. The mornings were now getting a little cooler and the gorse and heather had flowered and the grass now yellowed. For the first time this year, they noticed the dew that glistened on the strands of cobwebs stretched on the spikes of gorse.

As they walked downhill to the bridge over the stream their attention was drawn to a loud buzzing. A bee, out for an early forage, had become trapped in a cobweb. Bill looked around for a stick and quickly freed the bee.

'Good deed for the day,' he said to Beryl, as the bee flew away.

But then the bee was back, buzzing round the brim of Bill's hat. Bill could have sworn that a buzzy voice said, 'I'll return the favour.' Was it his imagination?

A few days later Beryl and Bill were just entering the usual car park in their little old car when the engine spluttered and died. Bill drew a breath.

'Umm, knew I should have filled up before we came. I'll just check the tank.' He walked round to the petrol tank and took off the filler cap. He was just moving to peer in when a bee buzzed past his ear straight into the tank. Another bee followed, then five, then ten more and then a swarm. There was a loud buzzing noise from the tank. Then one bee flew out, then another, then five, then ten and then the rest of the swarm. Bill was just standing back when a bee buzzed round his ear.

'Start the car,' it said – at least he could have sworn it said that.

Getting into the car again Bill announced in his most manly voice, 'I'll just have another try.' He turned the key and the engine sprang into life. He was about to close the car door when there was that bee at his ear again, buzzing words.

'That was the best "Bee Pee".'

I said that Beryl and Bill were an extremely loving couple but there was one silly little thing that always bothered Bill. On the top of the wardrobe there was an old chocolate box tied up with red ribbon. It had been there since they had moved in just after their wedding. Bill often asked Beryl what was in the box.

'My stuff. Just leave it, dear. One day …' was what she would always say. And Bill did leave it.

Time had passed since the bee incident and now Beryl and Bill no longer went for a morning walk because Beryl was ill and if the truth be known, she had not got much longer. Sitting by her bedside one day, Bill mentioned the box.

'Yes, get it down, dear,' she said. Bill reached for the box. 'Undo it and open it,' she said.

Bill took off the lid. Inside the box, at the top, was something wrapped up in tissue paper. He undid it. It seemed to be a stone entirely covered with multicoloured crochet.

'What's this?' he asked.

'Now, dear, I have to explain,' she said weakly. 'The day before we got married, my old mum said to me that whenever we had an argument, the best thing was to get a clean stone and quietly crochet over it to make a paperweight, and that is what I did.'

Bill looked at the stone paperweight. It was nicely made; multicoloured and neatly stitched, but there was only one. Only one argument? He reflected on their long marriage. One argument in all that time. He had been so lucky. He was about to put the lid back on the box when he noticed a brown envelope at the bottom. Beryl had drifted off to sleep now. He pulled out the envelope and looked inside. The envelope was stuffed with £20 notes – absolutely stuffed.

'Beryl, what is this?' he tapped her shoulder.

'Oh,' she said, 'there was never enough room for all the paperweights I made so I sold them at the WI stall. Those are the proceeds.'

I have stretched the notion of rock and stone a little in the first part of this story, but petrol is formed from decayed organic matter formed alongside coal in the Carboniferous layers of rock in the Earth's crust. It can be said to be a liquid fossil.

The Stonecutter

The Stonecutter is a widely told tale with many variations, though generally it carries the same philosophical message about greed and dissatisfactions that are not resolved and the message that it can be good to make the best of a situation. It may have its origins in China or Japan. It was collected by Andrew Lang in The Crimson Story Book *and story (1903) and a story with a similar morality is told by the Brothers Grimm ('The Fisherman and his Wife', 1812–1858). The same message is also played out in the hand game 'Rock, Paper, Scissors'.*

The stonecutter led a hard life. Each morning he said goodbye to his wife and shuffled out of his hut under the scraggy trees on the mountainside and made his way to the quarry. He hacked and sawed at the stone all day, his hands raw and his eyes and mouth filled with stone dust. Sweat dribbled down him. Then he trudged home.

Once a week he would hitch the mule to the cart and load the stone he had quarried and he would drive the mule down to the town, where he sold the stone to whoever needed it. This time it was a merchant who wanted it. He lived in a mansion at the edge of the woods and he needed it for a new summerhouse. As the stonecutter led the mule up the drive, he looked up to the little clouds in the sky and said to his mule, 'Why is it that my life is so hard? How I wish that I had a house like this with shady trees round it and other people serving me,' he mused, 'like a stonecutter bringing stone to me for my new summer house.'

A gust blew. It seemed that his mule spoke, 'Are you sure that is what you want?'

The stonecutter was a bit taken aback. He laughed at his own silliness.

'Of course,' he said.

And in that second, he found himself standing at the front door of a large house with a stonecutter coming up the drive. His wife joined him at the door.

For a while they led a lovely life, being known as the richest couple in the town, living in the big house, entertaining in the summer house at least twice a week. But by now as a rich man, he had made a few enemies too.

The day came when the rich man was sitting in his summer house, his feet up on a fine red velvet settee, trying to read his book. But the sun shone through the glass too powerfully. He was hot and it was too bright to see the pages of his book.

'Cursed be this heat,' he said. 'I wish I could be that sunshine.'

His wife looked at him from her chaise-longue.

'Are you sure that is what you would wish for, dear?' she said.

'Of course, I would like the power to over-heat and burn whoever I liked,' he said.

And he was that sun. For days he played with his power to heat and burn and he loved it. But once he had annoyed all those whom he wished to annoy, he became bored hanging about in the sky – and besides, the winter came and now clouds blocked his views and irritated him. But he did like the way clouds could bowl about the world, travelling high or low, it seemed.

'I wish I could be a cloud,' he thought (since no longer did he have a mouth to speak with).

'Are you sure that you wish for that?' whispered the creator into the sun's fires.

'Of course.'

And he became a cloud, loving the ability he thought he had to do what he wanted, where he wanted – to glower down on the world, to spew out rain, to cover everything with snow, to frighten people with thunder and lightning. But it seemed that every time he had chosen a target for some special weather, the wind blew him somewhere else. It blew him off the edge of the horizon for days, then blew him back to the mountains and he had just settled there when he was being gusted down into a valley.

'I wish I could be a mountain, then nothing could move me,' he said. 'I would be rock solid forever.'

'Are you sure that is what you want?' It was the mountain top that spoke. 'If so, come and join us.'

And he became a conical mountain that towered up and pierced feathery clouds.

'Ah,' said the mountain, 'this is perfect. I love it. I love the cooling cloak of snow that keeps me from the heat of the sun.'

Just then the mountain felt a tickling and pricking sensation in his lower slopes. Looking down, he saw a stonecutter going about his daily chores, chopping into the stone of the great quarry. He looked poor but he was humming as he swung his pick.

The mountain felt a tickling and pricking sensation in his lower slopes. He saw a stonecutter going about his daily chores.

'I wish I could be a stonecutter,' said the mountain. 'Then I could be simple and happy.'

And he became a stonecutter again and he was simple and he was finally happy.

Stone Soup

'Stone Soup' is a story that has been told all over the world, perhaps because it is a simple tale that is also clever in its outcome. The version here had origins in Hungary.

Gustav was on his way back to his homeland of Hungary after the wars. His clothes were ragged and he limped from an old injury, but his trusty pole helped him to wend his way along the forest tracks. And though he had few coins in his pocket, in his long days of travel Gustav had learned a thing or two about survival on the cheap.

The birds were roosting. It was towards evening and Gustav was getting hungry. He knew he was coming to a village as he could smell the smoke of the wood fires drifting through the trees. Though in the towns he could usually persuade some good wife or other to provide him with bread and cheese, in these poor villages, people usually had little to spare. Gustav began to look around on the track. He bent and picked up a large round stone and rubbed it on his jacket, turned it and rubbed again. The wooden huts of the village were coming into view. He collected a few sticks and headed for the centre near the pump and lit a small fire. He untied his pot from his pack and joined the evening queue at the pump for water. When he had filled his pot, very obviously he stood in front of everyone and dropped the stone into the water, put the pot on a grid over the fire and sat back with an air of contentment. Sure enough, people had watched him and were curious.

'What you doing there, boy?' asked a large woman with an even larger apron.

He lit a small fire.

'What yer making?' asked a small thin woman. 'You're not cooking a stone, are you?'

Others came over.

Gustav looked up.

'I am making the best soup in the world. Recipe's from the best cook in the country of France,' he said. 'Stone soup is delicious. However, I don't happen to have quite enough ingredients to flavour it properly. If I could – err – borrow maybe some little bits of vegetable to flavour it, that would be excellent. Mind, if someone would lend me a larger pot, then you can share it with me.'

A large cauldron was brought out, more sticks were brought for the fire and many handfuls of herbs, cabbage, carrots, potatoes, artichokes and parsnips, a little square of bacon fat, a strip of dried meat and a slice of sausage, all went into the pot. The stone rattled away, simmering amongst the rich flavourings for an hour. The baker came out with loaves left over from the day's bake. And Gustav served up the soup and bread for everyone, and the villagers ate with great enjoyment.

'Who would have believed that stone soup could be so good?' said the large woman, wiping her mouth with the apron.

'I'd like the recipe,' said the thin woman.

'Ah,' said Gustav. 'The best thing would be if I sold the stone to the village then you take turns to make the soup. Mind you remember the extra flavourings.'

The villagers bought the stone.

By dawn next day, Gustav was gone. Late on that day, smelling the smoke from the fires of another village, he picked up a nice round stone.

3

THE BIOGRAPHIES OF ROCK AND STONE

You look at a stone. You might say – 'Well it's just a stone.' But rock and stones have amazing stories to tell. They have come through amazing events. They have been in amazing histories, whether or not they have been touched by humans. And their stories will go on into the future, far longer than our stories.

The Tale of the Pinkish Pebble

I am drawn to pebbles that are distinctive or unusual and I have often wondered about the 'life' story of that particular pebble. Where has it been? Has it always been located in this place or has it moved? Has it had a part in the life of other human beings than me? The writing of this story below has been a matter of satisfying my own curiosity and extending my own knowledge. One of the things I came to appreciate as I wrote this story and the others in this section is an appreciation of the vastness of time – how for 4,000 million years, of Earth's age of 4,500 million years, not a lot happened except for the events of geology.

The tale of the pebble lurks in the hinterlands of both fact and fiction. The tale is about one pebble and not all pebbles. The stone in question is of a common material – quartzite. I chose to write about a quartzite pebble because these are an important component of the landscapes near where I live in Devon, the Pebblebed Heaths. What is unusual is that the surface ground of the Pebblebed Heaths is largely pebble, not earth. Agriculture has rarely disturbed the ground because there is not enough soil. And the pebbles are often distinctive. Locating the tale locally also allowed me to extend the story into some areas of archaeology that are familiar to me.

While this story is about one pebble, much of it would be true for other pebbles of different materials.

I used a number of books to write this tale, for example, Scriven (2016), Hart (2009) and Tilley (2017).

Naomi was walking on the heath with her family. They were on holiday from London, and were enjoying the sea air, as mother had said. There was an awful lot of sea air today, blowing strongly from the coast. They could see the greenish grey of the sea not far away. They walked along a pebbly track. Their black spaniel, Dilly, was racing ahead and ranging from side to side as usual. Naomi picked up a pebble. It sat nicely in her hand.

'Pinkish purple', she said, 'lovely colours.' She turned it over again. There was a patch of yellow and a whitish vein in it, which she traced with her finger. 'Where did it come from?' she asked anyone who was listening.

There was geological turmoil at the beginnings of the Earth as there was turmoil in everything. From the solar system, there was bombardment of debris. The rock that came to be the Moon may have broken away after a collision with another planet and earthquakes shook the Earth. Volcanoes pimpled all of the land. Unsurprisingly, one geological term for this period is the Hadean Eon. The time was around 4,500 million years ago.

Somewhere in the midst of this chaos a tiny volume of molten material that had been deep under the Earth's surface was spewed out of a volcano as white-hot magma. This tiny volume, or this cupful of material, is the heroine of this tale, eventually becoming part of the pebble in Naomi's hand. It was made of a common mineral, a form of silicon dioxide

Naomi picked up a pebble. It sat nicely in her hand.

that formed quartz crystals as it cooled. The crystals eroded to form grains of sand. Over the next few hundred million years through the vast Precambrian time period (with only the most basic life developing), the cupful of sand grains was pitched and crashed around on land, in water and underground. The grains were crushed together to form sandstone, heated to form quartz crystals and were eroded to sand grains again – and again. In terms of its location on Earth, the cupful moved as the great tectonic plates developed and started to shift. Around 250 million years ago, the cupful came to be located on a land called Pangaea, a continent comprising of most of the land masses on Earth at that time. Sitting on the land of Pangaea, it was then somewhere to the south of the equator. But tectonic plates were still moving and the sand or sandstone or quartz crystal – in these various states – shifted with them. The continent of America started to split from Africa and Europe and to shift north-westwards. Our cupful of rock came to lie on the land that eventually became France.

As the continents were pushed together and pulled apart by the tectonic plates, there was great heat and pressure. Land folded and refolded, was pressed beneath the surface, and heaved up again to create mountains. In this heat and pressure, the sand or sandstone coalesced to become hard rock that made up a range of mountains in northern France, in Brittany and Normandy, now north of the equator. The colour of the rocks varied as a result of staining, largely from different amounts of iron. There were colours of yellow ochre, pinks and purples and browns. The rock in this tale was stained pinkish purple, but in being laid down as rock, veins of purer white quartz cut across it. Life was beginning to happen more seriously at this time. It is possible that this rock might have contained fossils of primitive life forms, such as trilobites. As time went on, life became more sophisticated but there were stops and starts as massive periods of extinction occurred. But now the rock was accompanied in its time journey by different forms of life, small reptiles, tiny dinosaurs, large dinosaurs and many sea creatures.

Millions of years passed and the land continued to move, continually forming and re-forming. Through the actions of heat, frost, wet and wind, a chunk of this hard rock that was originally the cupful of sand or sandstone, eroded along with the rest of the rock of the French mountain range. It was washed into a great river that, around 240 million years ago, flowed across the land that bridged France and England at that time. The great river ran as a network of waterways over arid desert, northwards towards what would become the Midlands of the United Kingdom. This was in the Triassic period, when the climate was that of desert and periods of extreme wet.

The rock material, once the cupful of sand, rolled into this river as a craggy and uneven lump of rock but, through erosion by water and contact with other rock and sand, it became rounded. Some of it formed quartzite pebbles and some became sand again. The new pebbles and sand in turn played a part in eroding other rock and the pebble became more rounded the longer the time it was in the waters of the river.

And now there is a single pebble on which to focus – a pinkish purple pebble, with a patch of yellow ochre and a vein of white quartz. But it had not finished its journey. Land was still moving. The English Channel was being formed, and the land on which the pebble lay heaved upwards again to form heathland near to the sea in East Devon. The pebble was not still. It was washed in streams that formed during periods of flood, which then silted up, with the water taking different courses.

The pebble will never be still. All of these processes are still happening.

The great river ran as a network of waterways over arid desert.

But now the time is that of Homo Sapiens. The pebble came to lie in peaty earth on what would become the heathlands. There was not much disturbance of this land when Neolithic people were learning to till the soil for crops. There were just too many pebbles there and not sufficient soil. However, later during the Bronze Age, when people were starting to make metals, a couple of thousand years BC, the heathland was used as a site for rituals, the celebrations of births, pairings, deaths and other events. People built cairns of pebbles and the pebbles were specially selected for their colours and sizes. Two of these cairns were aligned with a distinctive hillside on the coast that had been a spiritual site for earlier peoples. The purple pinkish pebble was picked up from the bed of a stream by a man who sought pebbles for the cairn, but it was the wrong size and was discarded in another area of the heathland near to a track used by later people to cross the heath. Over the years it was picked up, admired and put down; scuffed by bare feet, feet in crude leather sandals, clogs and more recently shoes; picked up and put down, kicked by the hooves of horses and donkeys. And then it was picked up by Naomi.

Naomi took the pebble home with her to London where it sat on a shelf in her room until the family moved, and …

And the tale of the pebble will go on long after Naomi. The pebble may well become crushed back to sand and yet again re-formed or in other land movements, taken deep under the earth to become molten again.

The Tale of the Flint Stone

Often I find it hard to keep my eyes off the ground as there are so many interesting things to be found. It can be quite easy to pick up pieces of flint that have been worked (knapped) to form tools in the times of prehistory, more than 2,000 years ago. As long as I remember I have been interested in prehistory and the tools that people used. In recent times I have become more involved in archaeology and learning more about lithics has increased my interest.

Knapped flint is one of the main 'products' of early man. Knapping is the process in which flakes are removed from a block of stone, usually flint, in order to make a useful and useable product. Flint tools are common – they were made for many thousands of years before the discovery of metalworking. Gunflints were made for use in guns in the eighteenth and nineteenth centuries and flint can create such a sharp edge that it has been used in surgery even in much more recent times.

The knapping of flint is possible because of the manner in which flint fractures when it is hit. Below the point of percussion where the blow was directed, the flint fractures into a conchoidal form, a shell-like curved shape on one face. Further material is removed usually from the other face, to provide the final shape, though irregularities in the flint make this an unpredictable process.

And of course, flint stone has a longer history than the greyish/ brownish or black stone that might have been knapped all that time ago. It started millions of years before and that is where this story starts – over 100 million years ago in the Cretaceous time of the Mesozoic period.

Old Sandy sat on the log under these trees. He had always walked these woods, at first as a boy climbing the trees, then as a young man with one sweetheart or another on his arm. Later he brought his children, showed them the trees and pointed at those he had climbed and they climbed the trees or watched birds as they sung in the branches. Now he walked alone again and grieved for the love of his life. Absent-mindedly he picked up a stick, stroked the bark then reached forward for a piece of flint embedded into the earth of the woodland path. He eased the stone up with the stick. It had quite a sharp edge, a blade, and his hands almost automatically moved to use the blade to chip away at the stick. The action helped the pain of his mind. It took him back to his childhood and he thought of how time had passed for him. And he wondered on the passage of time for the piece of flint.

Around 145 million years ago, at a time when the continents of the Earth were still moving towards the way the world looks now, there was a great rise in sea levels. Many of the continents became covered by sea. On the land that was there, dinosaurs roamed.

In the waters there was a vast mass of small organisms with skeletons rich in calcium. As they died, they sank to the bottom and over tens of millions of years, their skeletons amassed eventually into white or grey chalk. The chalk sea was the environment in which the piece of flint, in the hand of the old man, had its origin. Calcium carbonate formed as the main chemical component in the water, but also there was silica and simple organisms, such as sponges and diatoms, which used the silica to create the structures of their skeletons. As they died, they sank onto and then deep into the chalk mud and a silica–rich liquid was formed. In chemical reactions deep in these sediments, which involved hydrogen sulphide, oxygen and carbonate, the silica precipitated to form the early stages of flint. Sometimes sponges or other organic remains formed a base for the formation of flint, so there can be the remains of fossils in flint. Or sometimes the chemical reactions took place in the burrows in the deep ooze and then flint nodules were generated in strange tubular forms that model the burrows in which the flint formed.

The piece of flint that Sandy used to carve the stick was part of a nodule of flint that had been formed in the burrow made by shellfish. The nodule was embedded in white chalk sediment in the south of what became the British Isles, though at that time England was still joined to France. There were periods of deep cold and then warmer times. Dinosaurs became extinct as mammals were, in a very slow way, starting to evolve. The chalk that formed at the bottom of the sea was pushed up by the movements of continents and dried as land. Where the land was highest, the chalk, being soft, tended to erode and flint nodules were exposed. The large nodule split into several still large lumps of flint. A neanderthal man picked up one chunk of flint and took it back to his base in a cave. He wanted to use it to smash the bones of a young mammoth that he had killed. He was hungrily seeking the bone marrow.

Thousands of years later in more recent prehistory, a family lived in the cave, sheltering as best they could from what was now a very cold climate. The nodule of flint still lay there. Where it had broken, it had lost the sharp edges and a whitish coating (cortex) formed like a skin over the cut face of stone. A Palaeolithic man picked it up and carried it to the log on which he sat when he knapped stone. He was an expert at knapping. With a rounded hammer stone filling his cupped hand, he struck the nodule to produce two pieces. He examined one piece and carefully selected how and where he would strike it again. Through carefully thinking ahead, he struck off flakes to form the rough shape of a large flint axe with two flatter sides. It had two

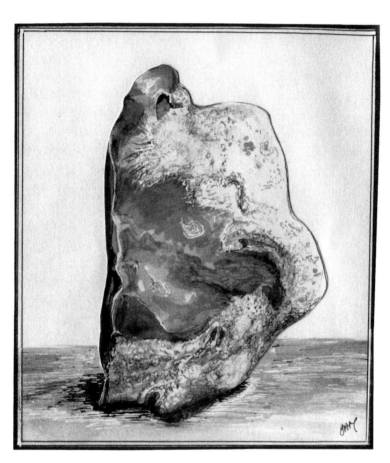

A nodule of flint.

Through carefully thinking ahead, he struck off flakes to form the rough shape of a large flint axe.

fairly sharp edges and a rounded end. He then retouched it with lighter strikes until he had sharpened the edges so they could cut through tough meat. The hand axe he had made was used by many people over the years. Sometimes more flakes were taken off to sharpen it again. And then it was lost on a hillside.

Thousands of years later the flint axe was found by Neolithic people who were preparing the ground for planting wheat. It had been made from a nice piece of flint and was knapped again, this time to form a number of blades and a scraper. The finer sharpening was done by using pressure exerted through the tip of a piece of deer antler. The scraper was used to clean flesh from deer skins for clothing and the blades were knives for cutting the deer meat. The best of the blades was retouched many times to maintain its edges until finally it dropped from a skin bag over a boy's shoulder and was lost.

The worked flint blade lay on the ground and soon was covered by fallen leaves, which, year after year, rotted to humus. For more than 2,000 years more it was buried, deeper and deeper. It was pushed around by the growth of the roots of trees and shrubs but then it was surrounded by the roots of a great oak tree, the largest tree in the wood. The oak lived for 500 years, but eventually rotted and fell, taking a huge root ball with it. The flint was in the root ball. Over time insects and fungi worked at the wood round the flint until it was earth again but now the blade was on the surface of a woodland path. The path was worn down daily by footsteps and horse hooves until the blade was once again exposed on the track of a green lane. In heavy rain the track formed into a stream and the stone was carried down by water and deposited face down. And old Sandy, grieving for his lost wife, found it and used it to chip at a piece of wood. And he got up and wandered home, dropping the flint tool as he stood. And the history of the flint continues.

The Ammonite Fossil

In some places the very ground itself is made up of fossils. Sometimes you can see them and sometimes they are too small. When we walk on chalk or limestone or where the ground is black with coal deposits, then we walk on fossils. In other places fossils are rare. Fossil-bearing rock can be too deep or the rock surface may have been formed before there was life that could be fossilised. Or the land may have been subjected to heat and pressure that destroyed the structures of fossils.

Ammonites are a common fossil in the United Kingdom because they thrived for a long period and those periods are well represented in UK geology. Ammonites were molluscs, related to the octopuses, squids and cuttlefish of today. They had a coiled shell and tentacles, gills and simple eyes and swam in the shallow seas, adjusting their buoyancy and where they swam in the water by taking in or expelling water from the chambers of their shell. They survived from around 200 to 65 million years ago in the Cretaceous period when, along with the dinosaurs, they died out in one of the great extinction events.

There are a number of legends that 'explain' fossils before there was the current understanding of their places in geology and evolution. I have referred to one such legend.

To write this story, I have drawn on Scriven (2016) and Hart (2009).

An ammonite swam through the warm Jurassic sea. It fed continuously on the shrimps that swam all around it and then it came to the end of its life and died. The sea was calm at the time and the ammonite sank to the seabed. It rested on the seabed for only a short time, as a storm blew up that stirred the waters. Sediment rose in great clouds and the remains of the ammonite quickly became buried. This burial was the most significant event in the process of its fossilisation. The soft parts of the ammonite decayed or were eaten, leaving the coiled shell deep in the sediment. Most shells would have filled with mud then been crushed, but the hollow spaces in the shell of an ammonite were filled with calcite and, in the case of this particular ammonite, also pyrite (iron sulphide), which had an effect on its appearance many thousands of years later. Over long periods of time crystals grew inside these spaces then the same chemicals infiltrated the material of which the shell was constructed and they replaced the material of the shell. A fossil was created. At the same time as the shell was becoming a fossil, the sediment in which it was embedded was subjected to pressure. It was compacted, and slowly became limestone rock. A large part of the sediment was made up of other shells now crushed beyond recognition and this made up beds of limestone.

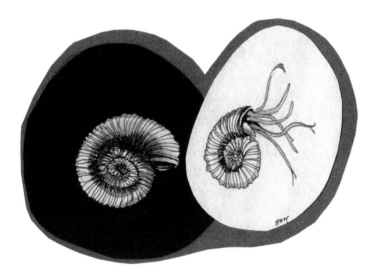

An ammonite. Ammonites had a coiled shell and tentacles, gills and simple eyes.

Over time the waters under which the rock lay receded, leaving the English Channel between England and France. The limestone in which the fossilised ammonite was embedded, formed the cliffs at the edge of the sea. The action of the waves and wind gradually exposed new rock. Water seeped down from the top of the cliff. In cold periods that water froze and cracked the rocks, and the cracks were widened when the hot sun of summers dried the land. In a great storm that part of the cliff fell to the beach in a small landslide and the fossil, still embedded in the rock, came to rest under tons of earth and other rock on the beach. The earth and rock debris was removed at every tide and there came a time when the ammonite fossil lay exposed. This was in late medieval times.

A man walked on the beach with his son. The son bent to look at the fossil.

'Don't touch that,' the man said. 'It be a snake turned to stone.'

The boy stood back. 'A snake?'

''Tis said that St Hilda, who founded our monastery, first had to cast out the snakes. She used her whip to take off their heads and turned them to stone and threw them over the cliffs onto the beach. This was one of the snakes.'

Later in the day the boy and some of his friends, somewhat curious about the stories, went back to the beach and with borrowed tools, gently broke the ammonite out of the limestone. Streaks of gold colour from the iron pyrites shone in the sun. The boy took it home. He continued to collect fossils and other interesting stones that he found on the beach and he carefully laid them out near his cottage. However, villagers told his parents that the fossils were the playthings of witches and should not be kept. The boy thought of hiding them elsewhere, but before he had time to do that, they disappeared one night, collected by the neighbours and thrown back into the sea.

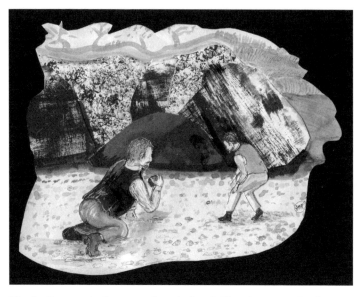

The fossil ammonite lay exposed on the beach. Then it came under the gaze of a fossil collector.

Over the years people talked about these strange stones that looked similar to modern creatures, but not exactly the same. There was a notion that they were very old but there was deliberation as to why God would have put them on Earth. Why were they there? Life was as it was. Perhaps God put them there as decorations for the humans to admire. Then in the 1800s there were stirrings of the idea around evolution. There was a suggestion that fossils were indeed a record of prehistoric and pre-human life on Earth. This contradicted the bible teachings about 'the Creation'. Charles Darwin's book, *On The Origin of Species* increased the controversy and argument.

The fossil ammonite lay exposed on the beach again and was picked up and mused over by those who passed it. Then it came under the gaze of a fossil collector. It was a particularly well-preserved and complete ammonite, and he carefully wrapped it and took it home. He displayed it in a great cabinet for years, and his visitors gazed at it through the glass. But the man aged and the glass became dusty. He died and his collection was put up for sale. It was bought by another wealthy man, but he did not get around to displaying it and it was stored for years in a dusty cellar. He died and his collection was bought by another who was setting up a fossil shop. The ammonite was brought into the light and cleaned. It was indeed an excellent specimen and it was displayed briefly before being purchased to sit on the mantelpiece in a pub. And there the ammonite resides, but its story is not complete. Where does the story go from here?

Tales from a Limestone Quarry

The tales below are real stories from the long history of the Quarry Caves at Beer in Devon. However, these kinds of stories could match those from other old limestone quarry workings.

The Beer Quarry Caves are an extensive network of man-made horizontal tunnels and chambers that wind through a substantial deposit of limestone. The stone has been quarried there almost continuously since Roman times and there are guided tours in the old workings during which the fascinating history and stories about the quarries are told.

Beer limestone was formed when, in the Cretaceous period, coccoliths (a form of unicellular plankton) died and drifted to the bottom of the sea and this sediment, under pressure, was transformed to stone. The limestone at Beer is particularly valued. While underground it can be cut by a saw and carved into desired shapes, and when in the air it hardens to a creamy white stone.

The tales were told to me by John Scott and his daughter, Karen Mynard. John was a founder of the group who saved the entry to the old quarry workings from being blasted, on the basis of the important and long history. I am very grateful to them for their time and for these fascinating stories of real lives. The caves are owned by Clinton Devon Estates and leased to Beer Quarry Caves Ltd.

Visitors enter the dark of the Beer Quarry Caves with a small group of others, all equipped in hard hats. A first experience in the summertime is the cold. In the winter the caves are warm as there is a constant temperature. Looking back from the darkness, you see the outside light through the several archways of different shapes and they represent the start of the stories. Roman, Saxon and Norman and later quarrymen worked the stone according to the architectural forms of their times.

So the Saxon archway is square, and the Normans worked with pillars. In Tudor times, there were Gothic arches. Further inside, lit by electricity, it is evident that the working was less rough as, in around 1700, saws came into use along with the pickaxe, hammer and iron wedge tools.

The Romans were first to find the limestone at Beer when they sought stone to build fine villas and military establishments here at the end of the Fosse Way. They probably saw the stone from the sea, noticing the white chalk of Beer Head. They tunnelled the horizontal limestone layers from a valley inland from the village of Beer and this is still the entrance to the Quarry Caves. Beyond quarrying, the Romans may have used the quarries for the worship of the Sun God, which required complete darkness. Finds in the caves such as a Roman brooch and coins may have been offerings, not careless losses.

The Beer Quarry Caves.

Since then the quarries have been worked almost continuously. The gap in working was in the reign of Henry VIII when, because of the Reformation, religious buildings were pulled down or taken into the ownership of the Crown. Towards the end of his reign, however, Henry built five cathedrals and there was again call for stone. During Henry's reign a secret chapel was set up in the Quarry Caves for illegal Catholic worship.

There was a strong need for Beer limestone too during the Victorian period, when many churches were built or modified. About 1900 new workings on the opposite side of the valley were developed because the tunnels in the old workings had become too lengthy for the horse-drawn wagons to bring out the heavy blocks.

Beer stone has long been associated with religious buildings. It was used in twenty-four cathedrals, including St Paul's, Westminster Abbey and Exeter Cathedral, and other significant buildings such as Windsor Castle. There is Beer stone in many Norman and Saxon churches. Sometimes what seemed like stone quarried for the construction of Saxon churches, on the inner faces, has been shown to have Roman inscriptions, so the stone was recycled.

From early Norman times, the Bishops of Exeter owned the rights to the stone in the quarry. This gave them a considerable means of earning money from its sale. In contrast to the wealth that the Bishops accrued from selling the stone, the local quarrymen earned less than farm labourers, and when there was no fishing, for many, quarry work was the only alternative. Children as young as eight toiled in the dreadful conditions of dust and extreme labour. The echoing noise of saw or hammer in the cave system would be constantly deafening. The quarrymen had to purchase the five candles a day that they used to light their corner of the pitch darkness. These candles were attached to the walls by red clay, the marks of which can still be seen. Sometimes the candles were attached to the helmets they wore, which were made of hardened clay and moleskin. Each man was expected to cut a four-ton block of stone in his fourteen-hour day, for six days a week. At the end of each day the Tapstone came round with a hammer and tapped each block. If the stone did not ring, it was deemed to be cracked and the quarryman would not be paid, though he would still have had to pay for his candles and this is the origin of the sayings that something is 'Not worth a candle', or 'Not worth a light'.

Detailed records of the workings were kept, and these can be linked to the signatures of those working in the caves. The men were taught to write their signatures on the walls to indicate where they had reached from one day to the next. The two categories of workers, quarrymen and stonemasons, wrote in different ways. The quarrymen wrote their names in charcoal black, the masons etched their names into the stone.

Stonemasons considered themselves to be the elite. Often they had to work beside the quarrymen, shaping the stone inside the quarries, as the high water content of the stone might have frozen outside in winter, causing it to crack when worked. The stonemasons protected their status by passing their right to work as masons down through their families or by setting up expensive apprenticeships that only the wealthy could afford. They also swore not to betray their trade secrets and this led to the development of Freemasonry. With one exception at Beer, no local boy in a quarryman's family ever came to be a stonemason.

The one exception is an interesting story. In 1801, William Cawley left home for work but he did not return home that night. It was assumed that he had, like many others, died in the dreadful work in the quarry. However, he had signed his

The quarrymen had to purchase the five candles a day that they used to light their corner of the pitch darkness.

name on the stone at the end of the day there. He had then done what many others did when they left the quarries and he engaged in the similarly tough work of smuggling. A diary entry was found that indicated that a fishing boat had landed that night and William Cawley died when a keg of brandy fell and broke his neck. For obvious reasons the cause of his death was to be kept quiet, and his widow went on to bring up their three children alone. The story of William Cawley re-emerged some fifty years later when William's widow took her first trip into Exeter. She went to the Bishops of Exeter and paid them the sum required for her grandson, another William Cawley, to take an apprenticeship to become a stonemason. The widow had been given the money by the smugglers because of her husband's death, and evidently had hidden it in her cottage for fifty years. An irony might have been that the money given to the worthy Bishops had been earned in smuggling – but then many of their kind in coastal Devon were quietly involved in just that same activity.

There are also some strange or ghostly stories associated with the caves. One day a guide, leading a party, opened his mouth to mention the historical events that occurred in a dark chamber to one side of the tunnel, when a young woman started to fall into a faint. Her husband caught her and when she had recovered, she said that she felt deep embarrassment as she had looked into the side chamber and had seen people in Tudor costume, kneeling to pray. The guide had been about to tell the party about the use of that chamber for the illegal religious services during Henry VIII's reign.

It is also said that visitors sense unseen children walking with them as they are guided through the tunnels.

Exploration of the caves is ongoing. Many areas are blocked by heaps of chalky waste. The material arrived in the cave system down shafts dug from the surface by workers who were taking chalk and limestone for processing in lime kilns. Two products of this process were limewash and lime cement that were used in the work of the stonemasons. When it has been possible to reach chambers beyond the heaps of waste material, there have been footprints in the stone dust that has now set like plaster on the floor. The footprints were made four hundred years ago.

4

SHAPES OF ROCK AND STONE

The grit that jumps into the back of your boot and rubs a blister, the mountain range that towers above you, the beaches that spread before you, the city skyscrapers: these are some of the shapes of rock and stone. Stones can be flat enough to bounce on water, they can have holes in them, faces carved from them, they can be sculpted into statues, or people can be turned to stone …

The Skimming Stones

The setting for this story is the reign of Elizabeth I in the late 1500s; times of suspicion and uncertainty in society, but also of exploration and the broadening of thought. I first thought of writing it when I saw some children and adults skimming stones on the Exe Estuary and I fell to thinking about how stones have been used in games and pastimes as long as people have enjoyed play. The choice of the setting is based on my research for Devon Boy 1590 *(Moon, 2017), a small book I wrote for the local history society in order to increase understanding of what it was like to live in a rural village at that time and then to get involved in sailing to Newfoundland to fish for cod during the summer months (2,000 miles across the Atlantic each way). Village life is the focus of this story.*

It was cold outside. Not surprising really, it was mid-winter. Wind rattled the shutters of the New Inn and draughts fluttered the flames. The small audience of villagers clustered as near as they could to the fire and pulled their shawls and cloaks around their necks. The light danced across their faces as they listened intently to the storyteller's tale. The storyteller had a strange but engaging voice, sometimes almost like that of a woman, but other times it was low and hard. He was small and his bright eyes sparkled through wisps of white hair that showed beneath a large hood, and his eyes told the story along with his voice.

This story was unusual. It was about a young girl called Carrie. The stories of most storytellers were about boys and men, lords and kings and princes and their occasional princesses – and Carrie was a country girl, living in a small cottage with her parents and now only one older brother, Thomas. Two other children had died and Carrie's sister was now working away at a farm on the other side of town, as a domestic servant. Carrie would move away in a few years too. She sorely missed her sister, who could rarely visit home. During the day Carrie and her brother would look after the family pig and the new litter, feed the chickens, weed the vegetable patch and scare away birds. In the evenings, Carrie had to help her mother to card raw wool that would be spun into yarn that was collected by the wool agent for a little bit of extra money. These things took most of Carrie's time.

Carrie's brother, Thomas, had many friends and after they had finished their work, the boys would sneak off to the edge of the nearby estuary to talk, jest and throw stones into the water. They tried to skim stones. Skimming stones and bouncing them on the surface of the water became competitive and Thomas quickly became good at it. On occasions, Carrie would go down and watch. Now the number of times the stone skipped on the water was carefully counted and noted in marks on an old piece of wood. One day Carrie drew up her courage and asked if she could join in.

Thomas shook his head. 'Girls don't do that.' He turned away.

'She could write the scores for us,' said one of the boys. There was no response from Thomas. Until recently, Carrie and Thomas had been close.

The boys learnt to pick out the stones that would skim best. They would try to put marks of ownership on them, but they could rarely find the better stones again because they skipped further and sunk beyond the low tide mark. Carrie still came to watch but now hid behind the boats pulled up on the shore. She watched how the best skimmers threw and how their stones shifted across the surface. She looked for flat stones. On occasions when she was sent to the shore to pick sea beet and find mussels for the evening pottage, when she was on her own, she tried skimming stones. She got better at it and her stones were bouncing four and five times.

It was the end of harvest time and the estuary villages celebrated with a fair, a day of games and festivities. A stone skimming competition was to be one of the games, with the men and boys competing against one another. Thomas had been practising for some time, and now spent time searching for good stones. Carrie had a small collection of excellent skimming stones and the day before the fair, she tentatively offered Thomas two of her best. Ruefully he took them from her.

On the day of the fair there was strong cider, music and dancing and stalls of sweetmeats and trinkets, and then the games. Everyone went down to the waterfront to watch the stone skimming competition. Thirty men and boys from all the villages took part. Thomas won and he was well congratulated for his skills and for the quality of his stones.

'Yes, they come from a secret place,' he said proudly.

The storyteller sat back as the innkeeper shuffled people out of the way when he came in with more wood for the fire. They moved reluctantly, not wanting to shift their attention from the story, but they shifted quickly when a mass of sparks flew.

The storyteller continued:

Carrie went on spending spare moments practising skimming the stones. Now she could often get a stone to bounce ten times, and to curve out and round and sink fairly near to the shore, from where she might sometimes retrieve it. But she only skimmed stones when there was no one else to see.

It was the time of the fair the following year and as usual, it was a great social event. There were often a few people who were strangers. For example, this time there was Marcus the Carter. No one knew him and everyone thought this lad must come from a village other than his own. Marcus was small.

'Strange lad, that,' said Thomas to his friends, as Marcus took his turn, 'but good.' The stone bounced impressively.

Thomas took his turn. People cheered. He had quite a reputation now, but Marcus had scored better and he won with his second stone. When the clapping died down and people had started to move, Marcus disappeared up the track. Ten minutes later Carrie joined the crowds, trying to show nothing of her pleasure at winning. But Thomas noticed she was different, and his suspicions were rising.

Marcus scored better and he won with his second stone.

For a few days after the fair there was talk about the mysterious Marcus. From where had he come? No one knew. Then someone remembered seeing a small figure scurrying away from the harbour. His old shirt was found under the hedge. It was recognised. There was talk, and Thomas challenged Carrie.

'It was you.'

'It was,' said Carrie, feeling both fear and pride.

Thomas flew into a rage. He had expected to win. He called her a cheat and railed against her in front of their parents. Their father was disappointed that his son had not won and was not willing to move his support to Carrie. As far as he was concerned, this was an activity for men and boys.

'If you do strange things,' said Thomas to her, 'people might think you are engaged in evil things. Just a warning.'

FOLK TALES OF ROCK AND STONE

Carrie turned away, uneased by his tone. What had been a peaceful family was now anything but that and she spent more and more time alone.

It was near the beginning of the New Year. The time had come for Thomas to leave home and work on another farm so the family no longer needed to support him. As the oldest child, this was usual. But the father decided that it would be Carrie who would be sent away. She was young but her presence was disruptive. And if there was any hint of strange behaviour, people would talk.

In early spring, Carrie was sent to the hiring fair in the town. She carried a duster to indicate the work that she was offering and she was hired by a Mr Wright, a yeoman of Seafield Farm. On the day before she left, Thomas took her aside.

'You're not just going away to work. You're being banished. Witches behave strangely like you.'

She looked hard at him and walked away.

The next day she left home with a crust and a piece of cheese for the journey, her Sunday best clothes and instructions to ask the way to the farm at the second coaching inn before the town walls. Carrie had always known she would leave home, but the way it had happened made her sad.

She arrived at the farm to be welcomed by the Wrights. Mr Wright was a large man who laughed. The farmhouse, to Carrie, seemed huge, with an outside chimney and ceilings. She had never been in a house like this. Her home had no ceiling and the smoke from the fire drifted up through the roof. Mary Wright showed her around. Carrie and the other servants slept in an adjoining barn on a platform over the animals, so at least it would be warm. Mary proudly showed off the two new glass windows. They would buy more glass when they could afford it. She introduced the other servants and described

Carrie's duties. She would help in the kitchen, clean, bring in wood and keep the fires in, milk the cows and feed the hens and sometimes do work in the dairy or in the garden. She would have a little time for herself after supper and she would have Sundays off after church. In return she would get a few pennies a day, and her keep. There were three other domestic servants who had been with the Wrights for a while and four male farm servants. Carrie was a lot younger than all of them.

The Wrights were kind to their servants. Carrie ate better than ever in her life, but she was perturbed by the sudden change and the loss of her friends. There was rarely going to be time to get home and back on foot on a Sunday so she took to walking the local lanes. On the third Sunday she came down through a wood and discovered a large lake. Almost absent-mindedly she picked up a stone and tried to skim it. It was far too rounded but on her way back, she passed by a small quarry with flatter stones. From then on she went to the lake whenever she could and on each visit she would seek stones to skim across the water of the lake.

It was twilight one evening after supper. Carrie was skimming stones on the lake, thinking of the days at home and wondering how her family would receive her if she could get home. She was reaching for another stone when there were voices. Shyly she looked round. Jed and Peter, two of the farm servants had evidently been watching her and they sauntered to the shore, picked up some stones and tried to show her that they could do better. Stone after stone sunk. It was not long before one of them sidled up to her.

'Come on Carrie, show us how.'

Within a day or two, all the farm and domestic servants were collecting stones from the quarry and then spending time on the beach learning to skim them. A few days more and Mr Wright, concerned about the enthusiasm of all his servants for the trip to the lake, followed them down and soon joined in. There was jesting and laughter. These were happy days for Carrie and she was proud to be at the centre of attention.

It was coming up to the Feast of Fools, just after Christmas. As was usual for this festival, neighbouring villagers were entertained to a meal of roast goose and festivities at the Wrights' farm. Jed was selected to be Lord of Misrule to direct the games, merriment and fooling. In the traditional way, the Wright family dressed as servants and served the food. Carrie was taken aback when Mr Wright addressed her as 'Mistress Carrie' and then she and the other domestic servants were hitched to the donkey cart and the farm dog was placed in the seat of the cart. Everyone laughed.

Then, urged on by Mr Wright, Jed announced a stone skimming competition and everyone paraded down to the lakeside, picking up two stones each at the quarry. Carrie's stone bounced eleven times and skidded on before sinking. There was cheering. No one else managed more than eight bounces. The copious strong cider may have helped or hindered everyone's activities. Possibly more important for Carrie's technique now was the way she knelt on one knee as she spun the stone. Others tried to bend down but soon gave up.

Spring brought sun and warmer weather. The boys were busy lambing and the domestic servants helped to plant the kale, parsnips and herb seeds. Carrie had not visited home because she was happy staying at the farm on a Sunday. The occasional news came back from people who knew her village. There were suspicions about old Eliza. Someone had accused her of being a witch and causing others to become ill. As a result, villagers were busy carving the 'W' symbols on their doors to deter witchcraft. Carrie was sad about Eliza. She had been a kind woman and in the past Carrie had spent time with her. It was a shame that she had turned out to be a witch.

May was coming. Mr Wright loved festivities and he had long been involved in setting up the May Day fair at the harbour of the nearby town. The servants had a day off and Mr Wright had made a special point at supper the day before of suggesting they all should select some good stones as there would be a stone skimming competition. Carrie knew the fair and knew that the stone skimming competition there had been open only to men and boys.

'It is not a problem,' said Mr Wright. 'You will take part. We'll make sure.'

On the day of the fair, the servants walked alongside the Wrights and their family who were driven by Jed in the cart. Nell, the best of the farm horses, drew the cart, her coat gleaming and the harnesses polished. Everyone was in their best clothes. Children sung in groups and danced around with flowers in their hair. Carrie was nervous about the competition. Thomas would probably be there. Early on she saw him talking loudly with a group of friends. He was taller now and he spoke with the arrogance of someone expecting to win. The stone skimming contest was to be at the hour of three. Competitors gathered, clutching their precious stones or fingering them in leather pouches. Onlookers moved from the maypole dancing and stalls to watch. Thomas saw Carrie and he strode over.

'What are you doing here?' His voice was hard. Anger flashed in his eyes.

For Carrie, memories came back. 'The contest –'

'It is not for girls. You were told that.'

Carrie tried to explain. 'Mr Wright –'

But Thomas stormed away and his friends clustered round him, periodically looking towards her.

A few minutes later there was a call for the competitors to gather on the low area of the quay. The farm servants from Seafield urged Carrie to come along with them. She hesitated, clutching her two stones nervously. There were no other girls taking part and people were pointing at her, talking about her. Now it was her turn. She was shown the throwing spot. She crouched to throw and just before the stone left her hand, her arms were grasped from behind.

'Crouching like a toad, girl. You don't even need a familiar – you are one.' There was jeering and laughter. A tall, official-looking man looked down at her.

'We hear you spent time with Eliza, the witch, so we know where you got it from.'

Carrie was dragged away through the crowd. People jeered before they parted to make way. At the back of the crowd, Mr Wright caught up. There was fierce argument and Carrie could hear him attesting to her innocence. Then Mary Wright was there. Carrie was deeply frightened. She saw Thomas looking satisfied. However, Mr Wright had influence and Carrie was released. She was bruised, shocked, and bleeding. Mary led her quietly away from the crowd.

'They are saying you are a witch. We see you as innocent. You can tell us the story later, but the boys will take you back to the farm where you will be safe – for the time being.'

Jed and Peter helped Carrie into the cart and Jed picked up the reins. Back at Seafield farm, while Jed drove the cart back, she sat on the bench with Peter, slopping the small beer from the bowl in her shaking hands.

'I don't believe you are a witch either.' Peter broke the silence.

'I don't even think my brother believes that. But it is useful for him to say it,' she said. 'Winning's all that matters.'

Late in the evening, the merrymakers returned from the fair, tired and smiling. Mary came over to the bench and put her hand on Carrie's shoulder.

'A very bad thing your brother did to you,' she said. 'You are not a witch. But we must talk tomorrow.'

'He won?' asked Carrie.

'He won.'

The next day Carrie sat by the fire with Mary.

'We have been talking,' Mary said. 'It would not be good for you to stay on here, for your sake and ours. People heard your brother and will want to believe him. These are bad times, with plague back in the town and the poor harvest last year. People will blame you.'

Carrie had expected this.

'So you must go, though that makes us sad.'

The storyteller sat up straight on the stool and looked round the listeners, then looked into the glowing logs of the fire.

'So you'll be wondering what happened to Carrie. In three days, she left Seafields Farm,' he went on. 'The Wrights arranged for her to travel with one of the traders who visited the farm. She went to a farm owned by Mr Wright's brother and his wife. They knew her story but others did not. She worked as a domestic servant for several years. After getting over the terrible accusations of her brother, she was happy again and made friends, but the events still bothered her. She knew well that often the stinging accusation of witchcraft was a neat means of a man achieving his goals by getting a woman out of his way.

'Slowly and very tentatively, Carrie started telling her story to close friends, without admitting it was her story. She gained confidence and told the story at local farms and villages.

Her story slowly stirred talk in families. There were women accused of being witches in every community, but still Carrie did not say it was her story.'

The storyteller suddenly stood from his stool and pushed back his hood. The grey hair came away with the hood and revealed a mass of brown hair. He untied his cloak and as the black cloak heaped on the floor he stood straight. But it was a woman standing there.

'For the first time I tell you, who listen.' The storyteller seemed to look everyone in the eye at the same time. 'I am Carrie. I am not a witch. Story is truth and it is wisdom.' She paused and looked around again. 'Think on it.'

The Adder Stone

This story is from Lewis in the Outer Hebrides off the Scottish coast. I first saw a version of it in a book by Moira Miller (1990). Looking into it further, I discovered that it relates to some degree to a network of legendary stories about a man called Coinneach Odhar, sometimes referred to as the Brahan Seer (Brahan is a place near Inverness). He may have lived in the seventeenth century. As a seer, he could look into and predict the future and according to the legend, while he became well known for his successes, he may also have come to a bad end. For this version of the story, I have drawn on a number of sources including the Reader's Digest *(1977) for references to adder stones.*

Over many centuries, as also today, people have lived in crofting communities in the highlands and islands of Scotland. As crofters they had a small cottage and a patch for growing their own vegetables, and they had animals, usually sheep, that grazed on jointly owned land. Income was supplemented in various ways. The women would card, spin and weave or knit wool and the men might fish in small boats on lochs or the sea.

Long ago there was a group of crofters of the MacKenzie clan on the island of Lewis. Maggie and Jamie were among them and they had recently married. Like others they struggled to make a living. Both came from crofting families whose ancestry stretched back longer than anyone could remember. Like their fellow crofters they were proud of their heritage and when they found they were expecting a child, they naturally considered naming him Kenneth after the earlier Kenneths among Jamie's ancestors. They were completely agreed on this until the day when Maggie went down to the beach to bring back the sheep, where they were eating the seaweed.

Storms were expected. Purple-black clouds were already rolling in across the sea. It was the time of sunset and between the
clouds, the occasional ray of gold sunshine fell across the beach.
Maggie walked awkwardly across the foreshore as the baby was
due soon. She loved looking at the colours of the pebbles and
often picked one up, enjoying its cool roundness in her hand.
But this time, one pebble, lit beautifully by the sun, caught her
eye. This one had a hole through it. Idly she pushed her finger
through the hole. The pebble was like a big stone ring. She
remembered that her granny once called a stone like that an
adder stone and she had said it has powers – but granny also
said that a black cat crossing the path was lucky, just as Maggie
tripped over it and grazed her knee.

Maggie was fingering the stone and reflecting on the memories. She held it up to her right eye and looked out over the
gold, blues and purple of the stormy sunset. Then she held it
to her left eye. At first she saw little, but then she felt a strange
warm vibrancy, and when the view cleared it was not as she
expected. There were square blocks that might be huge cottages and an enormous ship in a busy sea, and people dressed
oddly. She took it from her eye quickly, unsettled by the
experience and at first she could only see blackness from her
left eye and then strangeness seemed to affect the baby as he
started to kick vigorously inside her. Feeling very uncomfort-
able, Maggie quickly caught hold of the first of the sheep with
her crook and started to herd them towards their croft. She
could only think of lying flat down on her bed. She dropped
the stone and thought no more about it. But it was after that
that she started to have a different attitude to the baby. When
the question of his name came up again that evening, and
Jamie referred to 'our Little Kenneth', she sat up and said,
'No – I don't want to name him after your family. He will be

different. He will be known as a great man by people all over Scotland.' Maggie surprised herself with what she had said, and yet it felt right. Yes, she did want her baby to be different, powerful and not just a crofter.

Jamie was a man of tradition and he stood back in amazement. He straightened.

'Being a crofter is a most honourable way of life. I am proud. He will be proud to be one of this family.'

I need not give details of the long discussions that followed – and it was quite soon after that that the crofters of the area were celebrating with Jamie and Maggie the birth of their baby son who was to be named Kenneth, after Jamie's family.

'But he will be different – a man of power,' Maggie said to everyone whether they listened or not.

As people do, the gathered friends looked for likenesses between baby Kenneth and his parents. Hair, nose, eyes … he did look different. He was dark, with hazel eyes. Jamie was fair, but then some noticed that Maggie herself was darker in colouring than most of the other crofters.

And as the years passed, Kenneth grew slowly. He was small and stocky – not like his friends. Nor did he spend a lot of time with the other boys, playing catch or kicking the bladder of peas. He would more often be watching birds by the shore or in the blackthorn scrub, or he would be staring out to sea. Neighbours noticed and gossiped about it behind their closed doors. A changeling? A throwback?

It bothered Jamie that his son did not seem to be keen on joining him on fishing trips and would only reluctantly help with the milking the cow or moving the sheep. It did not help that Maggie kept talking about how Kenneth was developing into a man of power. Jamie would say, 'It's no good, Maggie, he's got to make a crofter's living. There isn't anything else.'

And Maggie would turn her head away angrily. But secretly she began to wonder how it might be that this little child could develop into the powerful and influential man that she imagined.

In the summer the women, with the children, would take their sheep and cows to the higher ground where there was better grass for some days, leaving the men to fish and tend the crofts. The women would live together in a hut or a shieling, and during the day, when they were not tending the animals or the children, they would spin wool, knit, sing and talk. Spinning was a gentle activity using a distaff, round which they wound the carded (combed) wool, and a spinner that would twist the raw wool into yarn. The warmth of the summer months was always a very special time for them but this year, the year of Kenneth's seventh birthday, Maggie was restless.

'Sit down woman, no sooner than you've sat but you're up again,' the other women would say. 'Could it be that there's another bairn on the way?'

Maggie would shake her head and wind more wool onto the distaff and stand up again. The restlessness was bad enough in the day, but at night she was sleepwalking. She had woken at the door of the shieling twice now and several times had disturbed Kenneth from his sleep as she fumbled back to bed, still asleep.

One night towards the end of the summer, after a particularly restless day, Maggie's sleepwalking took her out of the shieling and it was the cold of the dewy grass that woke her. It was before the sun rose but she felt too wakeful to sleep again. She reached inside for her blanket and picked up her crook, which went everywhere with her. It felt right to be out walking in the grey morning light and the path took her down to the group of ruined cottages by the little loch. It was cold as she went down the hill and there was mist over the loch. Nothing moved.

She sat on the low wall by the graveyard. The church building was gone and gravestones were fallen this way and that. It was as she sat that she noticed something strange. By most of the gravestones there was a split in the ground. Only once she saw these holes did she also notice how the mist was shifting in a strange way above them, twisting and stirring as if echoing the movement of people that she could not see. She would think she could see a face, then it would be gone. Thin ribbons like rainbows wound in and out of the mist. Maggie was scared. Then she was terrified, shaking – but it seemed too that the world around her was vibrating. Surely these were ghosts. She started to get up but then imagined that the mist shapes were swimming towards her and she sat back again, wrapping the blanket tightly round. Perhaps this horror would go if she could get back to sleep. She buried her head into the blanket for what seemed an age.

When Maggie looked up, most of the misty shapes had indeed gone and the ground was just the dewy grass of the early morning, no holes. The sun was now beginning to lighten the sky over the islands out at sea. She must have been dreaming, though the strange shakiness – that was still there. She picked up her crook and scrambled to her feet to walk back and then noticed that there was one grave that was still open. It was near the foreshore, an old grave supposedly of a Danish girl. Something stirred in Maggie's mind. She and the other women had been talking about it the other day as they walked past the graveyard. One had been saying that if you could help a spirit to find rest, the spirit would owe you a tribute. They had laughed and joked about how it would be to be granted a wish by a ghost. But this thought now drew Maggie towards the girl's grave. Maggie had a desire for the future of her son that desperately needed fulfilling. She crouched by the grave and carefully laid her crook across the split in the ground and waited. The rays of sun were just appearing and only faint wisps of mist hung above the grass. Then it was as if a patch of mist in front of her thickened and darkened as if infused with the rainbow colours she had seen earlier. The shape of a girl materialised, the features of her white face obscured by flowing hair. Then there was a far-off voice.

'Please let me back into my grave.' With every word, the appearance became stronger and though all was still around Maggie, the girl seemed to be standing in strong wind, her gown and blonde hair floating about her.

Maggie put her hand on the crook to steady herself and sat back again.

'Who are you?' she asked. To her surprise, her voice felt cool and calm.

'I am the spirit of a drowned soul. Please allow me to take my rest again or I will be forced to roam for ever.'

Maggie hesitated, feeling sorry for the girl.

'Tell me more about you then I will let you back.'

'I was a wild girl, different from all the others, loved to run away. One day the waters took me.'

'So now,' Maggie was leaning forward, 'if I am to let you back, I will ask a favour of you.'

The girl nodded. 'You have the right to do that, but please be quick.'

'My son, Kenneth. I want him to become a man of power, known by all people in our land.'

'That will be as you wish. Please clear my way. I will tell you from my place of rest. What powers do you wish for him? Quick – tell me now.' Her voice was fading fast.

Maggie lifted the crook from the grave and even before she had laid it down again, the substance of the girl seemed to melt into the orifice of the grave leaving only faint whiteness hovering in the air. Maggie cursed that she had lost the opportunity but the voice came again, like a deep echo.

'Now tell me.'

'I have thought on this. In crofting we work from day to day and are governed by the seasons. I would like him to break from this rhythm, to see the times ahead.'

'What you wish for may not always bring happiness. I warn you of this.' There was a pause. 'You, Maggie MacKenzie, once had the chance of this power but you threw it away and it has left you with a yearning over all these years to give power to your son. So be it.'

'So what do I do?' Maggie was sitting up.

'Go to the beach to where the sheep gather. Walk across the pebbles as the sun rises over the horizon and it will strike the adder stone that you discarded those years ago. You will know it. Give it to your son when he is of an age to use it wisely. Looking through the hole in the stone with his left eye, he will see things yet to come. Do not try it yourself.'

Maggie was on her feet.

'Farewell.' The voice was scarcely audible. 'And beware of this power you wish on your son.'

It was some days before Maggie was to be down from the shieling. She said nothing of her experience to the other women. Her sleepwalking ceased and it was as if, whispered the others to each other, she had a glow inside her. On occasions when she was alone with Kenneth, Maggie would smile wistfully, stroke his dark hair and murmur, 'You are to be different, son, just as I always said.' But then the boy had no understanding of these words.

On the first morning back at the croft, Maggie was out on the beach at sunrise, but there was thick cloud. The next morning was brighter and as the sun rose its rays struck the beach and there was indeed one pebble on which the light seemed to focus. It fitted her finger just like before. In her excitement, she held it to her right eye and saw the sheep wandering in a line down the shingle bank towards her. And then she held it to her left eye. There was a man with greying dark hair bound in irons, being dragged along a road by others in some sort of uniform. It was frightening and only then did she remember the advice of the Danish girl not to look through it. Rapidly she pushed the stone into her pocket but noticed that she could not see as well as before with her left eye.

There was indeed one pebble on which the light seemed to focus.

At home she hid the stone away. With a sense of satisfaction, but still with damaged vision, she got on with her life as a crofter and no longer said anything about Kenneth's destiny. Jamie was relieved.

When Kenneth was 16 he had the opportunity to work with another crofting community on the mainland for a short while, to learn some new crofting skills. As he was about to leave, Maggie took him aside and gave him the stone.

'This will change the course of your life, son. It may mean that you never return to us – but please remember where your life started.'

She asked him not to use the stone until he reached the new place.

A month went by then a traveller brought news to Lewis of a half-blind young man who seemed to be able to see into the future through his blinded eye. He had already saved chickens from attack by the foxes and his prediction of an unseasonable storm had encouraged the early harvesting of oats. This had saved the farmer a fortune. Maggie was deeply proud, though Jamie did not understand. They later heard that the man had been taken into the employment of Lord Seaforth of Easter Ross and was meeting with the famous people of the day. As well as predicting events of the next few days or weeks, he predicted Scottish battles of the distant futures. He became wealthy. It was when packages of coins came back to Maggie and Jamie that Jamie believed it was really Kenneth who had these powers.

But after another year there was another story. Lord Seaforth was married to Isabella, who was widely held to be one of the least attractive women in the islands. Lord Seaforth was away a lot and it seemed that the looks of his wife therefore did not matter too much. One day he had been overdue from a trip to France. Lady Isabella was getting anxious and she asked Kenneth to find the whereabouts of her husband. Kenneth lifted the stone to his blind left eye. He saw Lord Seaforth walking arm in arm with a beautiful woman dressed in the French style. He reported to Isabella that Lord Seaforth seemed to be in fine health and he was sure to be home soon. A day or two went by and Isabella demanded again that Kenneth should look. The view this time was of Lord Seaforth in the boudoir of the lady. He hesitated, not sure what to say. Isabella's face darkened and she became wildly and violently angered, taking the anger out on Kenneth. She threatened him, then she called in her bodyguards and announced that Kenneth had attacked her and that he should be taken away in irons. No more had been heard about him. As the sad news was told to Maggie, Maggie remembered the vision she had seen through the adder stone and from that moment, she realised that it was her ambitions that had led him to this end.

Coinneach Odhar was said to have foreseen the Battle of Culloden (1745) and to have said that one day Scotland would have its own Parliament again. Some legends suggest that he threw the adder stone into a loch when he knew that he was not going to live much longer, and it is still there for someone else to find.

Seeds and the Statue of Little Simon

This is a story about things changing and yet still staying the same. I wrote it a long time ago and then the focus was the game of seeds. In the current rewrite, the stone of the statue dominates. I wrote the story when there was the early consciousness of environmental destruction, when we heard about the rain forests being cut down in South America. The scene in the story of the forgotten garden seems in my mind to be associated with a childhood picnic in the Surrey countryside, by a small pond. It was a hot day and there were many beautiful dragonflies around. The bells from a nearby church struck midday. I think there is also some inspiration from The Secret Garden *by Frances Hodgson Burnett (1911).*

This story starts long ago. Little Simon was the fifth son of the Edwards family. Dr Edwards had done well in work and the family moved from a town house to a larger country house. The new garden was a particular joy to the children, with so much to explore and as long as they did not disturb the gardener, they were free to run in the trees and play with hoops and balls on the large lawn. It was so different from the hustle and limitations of the old life in the town. But that applied to four of the children. Little Simon was unable to run. He could hobble with a stick but often he was ill and he would be kept in bed. When he could be outside, he loved to sit by the lily pond and watch the dragonflies, pond skaters and coloured fish. The flowers of the lilies were beautiful. As time went on he got no better and at the young age of 6, he died. His death brought much sadness. A formal funeral was held and he was buried in the churchyard of St Thomas's Church.

'But we want something of our own to remember him by,' said one of the children, tears welling in her eyes again. 'We miss him so much. The garden isn't the same without him, sitting by the lily pond.'

'Perhaps we could we have a statue of Simon by the lily pond,' suggested her father.

Soon after that, a stone sculptor was commissioned to make a small statue of Simon. The creamy limestone would come from the nearby quarry. When the statue was completed a carter was sent to collect it and the statue was brought to the lily pond and placed in amongst waterside plants but it was too small.

'Little Simon can't see the pond,' said one of the children.

'We'll get the sculptor to make a pedestal for him then,' said Papa.

The pedestal was a hollowed out base and now Little Simon could look out over the pond in all the seasons.

Time moved on and life became hard for the family. It took a lot of money to look after the large house and the Edwards could no longer afford the gardener. The garden became overgrown and then the house fell into disrepair. The children left home and Dr and Mrs Edwards moved to a little house in the town. They were unable to sell the large house and weeds now grew in the gutters. Water overflowed and then wet dripped through ceilings. Over years, the house collapsed in on itself and nobody wanted it. It became a crumbled mass of red sandstone rubble with a few walls around the old fireplaces, surrounded by wilderness. Plants sprawled and crawled. Pink valerian pushed stones further apart, ivies clung. Ferns sprouted like green fountains and a sycamore grew in what had been the kitchen doorway. There were some old garden plants, such as raspberry, freed from the constraints of the gardener's hands and only conforming to the laws of the wild. Scented roses wavered away from the remains of a trellis arch, competing with the prickle of a large gooseberry bush. And everywhere, bramble was waving its long tentacles out to colonise new areas.

Of course, all this was good for wildlife. Insects, birds and animals abounded. Butterflies clustered on buddleia; bees droned in the sunlit areas and flies zipped across the patches of shade. By night, foxes chased rabbits and a badger had burrowed his way through the fragrant soil of what had been the herb garden. Perhaps those with a lingering right over the land were a family of cats that were descended from Jemima, a gentle tabby that had been fed by the last kitchen maid to work for the Edwards.

Another remnant of the life of the house was the statue of Little Simon, still sitting on the hollowed pedestal in a marshy area that had been the lily pond. The side of him in permanent shadow was greened with moss.

As with all remote and wild places, the spirits of the wood had moved in. Humans, in their ignorance, have called these elves, fairies and little people. But humans can be stupid. They tell stories of these spirits to younger children, while at the same time mocking the older ones who still believe. The spirits dwelled in the root spaces beneath the tall trees, in the high canopy of leaves and in the dark of hollow trunks that had been the play-places of the long-ago children. The spirits revelled in the breezes, shaking the branches as they danced to the music of summer twilight.

Late summer was a special time for these spirits. They would come from far and wide to the old garden where they played the game of 'seeds'. It was a game like 'conkers', the same as children play with the fruit of the horse chestnut, but the spirits played it with seeds and the string was spun cobweb. The seasoning of the seeds to be used in the games was a highly regarded skill. The seeds had to be hard but not brittle and burnished to a shine.

Late summer was a special time for these spirits. They would come from far and wide to the old garden where they played the game of 'seeds'.

Just the conditions for this treatment were found in the hollow in the base of the statue and over the years the hollow had become filled with woodland seeds. Or it might be just that the canny squirrels had made this their food store.

And so the wilderness rested over the years and, but for the occasional lovers from the village who sought the peace of the deep shade, no person entered.

However, as happens in the modern day, the land was spotted by a man who was interested in making money. He pursued his interest until he bought the land and then he laid out plans for buildings. One day, late in the summer, the sound of chainsaws came, ripping at fresh wood. The trees shuddered deep to their roots. As men tramped through the land of the old garden and used fires to destroy the undergrowth, all life that could move, fled. Birds ceased to sing, rabbits ran to new burrows and the woodland spirits thrashed around, disturbed and angry and then, on a day of high winds, they disappeared.

Soon the men reached the site of the house, carted away the old stone and razed the land on which it had stood. A digger knocked the statue of Little Simon into the mud that had been the lily pond and it was buried further by a mound of earth, pushed in on top.

In a day or two, more men came with tanks on their backs and sprayed chemicals over the ground to rid it of the vestiges of the wild. The remaining plants drooped and died as everything was destroyed. Trenches were now dug and foundations put in. There was noise. Houses went up – red brick, square houses with new brass knockers and tarmac drives.

The people who came to live in the house that was built over the site of the old lily pond, were themselves old. They had time to be keen gardeners. They abhorred weeds and removed even the cooling mosses that softened their lawn. The garden was dug, hoed, sprayed and raked. The edges of flowerbeds were cut sharp and the faces of the flowers glowered out, colourful but pompous. They were from the garden centre and they were expensive.

These people had grandchildren who would make occasional visits. The children lived in a city flat and the garden was a great source of joy to them, especially the gap between the wood fence at the end and the shed. Their grandfather could not get to this area because of his cumbersome garden tools and his arthritis.

'Don't let your ball go on the garden bed now, will you? Don't break the flowers,' the grandmother would say as the children went out. But they were used to those kinds of prohibitions from their life in the city.

One Easter, when the children arrived, a section of the vegetable garden was newly dug.

'Surely we can go on that bit of earth, and dig?' said the boy with a look of hope. The old man ruefully agreed.

'Let's dig a pond,' said the girl. They started to dig down, but did not get very far before they struck something hard. Sparks flew from the spade. As they cleared the soil, a face began to appear and the eyes of Little Simon stared up. They wanted to rush in and tell everyone but halfway to the door they slowed and, nearly together, stopped.

'Let's hide him and keep him as ours so that we can see him each time we come here,' said the girl. They dragged and pulled the statue down the path towards the secluded space behind the shed and as they did this, seeds, hidden so long ago, fell from the base.

'I'll wash him,' said the girl and she ran up to the house and struggled back with Grandad's yellow bucket, slopping water onto the newly scattered seeds as she went. The children spent even more time in the garden, now that they felt that they owned a small part of it.

'How they enjoy my garden,' said Grandad, thinking of his floral display.

The children went home. Spring came and warmed the earth even behind the shed and the seeds sprouted and grew and came into flower without anyone knowing. In the summer, the children were back, but this time everyone was sad because Grandad was very ill and could no longer tend the garden. The new plants flourished and spread and the statue was once again surrounded by growing things. While the grown-ups were deep in their worried conversations, the children played around the statue and the wild things in the garden.

Three months later the family arrived for the last visit. They came with a van brimming with furniture. They were now moving into the house and their grandparents were going to live in a flat.

'Look,' said their father, 'it's a big enough garden for all of us. You two can have the end part and do what you like with it. We'll try to keep the top half tidy.' The children danced with delight.

It was more than a year later. The sun had shone for weeks but not at its hottest as it was now autumn. A mouse scuttled through the undergrowth at the bottom of the garden, shaking stems and then abruptly changing direction as it came face to face with a large shiny black beetle. A bee buzzed around a yellow flower. And in among the stems and leaves, other forms raced and darted, collecting seeds and carrying them to the hole in the base of the statue. The next summer, in the dusk, with seeds carefully threaded onto spun cobweb, the games were back in play. And even in this small place, the spirit of the wild lived on.

The Face in the Rock

This is a story from North America but is not a Native American story. It is set in an area of rocky mountains and forests and has something of an alpine feel to it. My original source was a book called Great Stories from Many Lands *(1936). In that book it was collected and rewritten for children by Stella Mead. Mead's rewriting gives the stories rather a moralistic tone. In rewriting it myself, I have modified the original to strengthen it as a story and I have dropped some of the moralistic bits. The story attracted me at first more for the imagery that it promotes than the storyline itself. It takes me back to a time I spent on a fairly remote island on the west coast of Scotland (Sanda). I spent time wandering there, finding caves and rounding up sheep. I found several interesting things – for example, a prehistoric worked bone tool and stalagmites. Then I was shown a hidden area of cliff in which there is a face rather beautifully carved in the rock. It is of human proportions. It was not known who had carved the face, but from the style of the carving, possibly it was someone who had had experience of stonework on churches and cathedrals. The face in this story is much, much larger! I imagine the story to be set in the 1800s.*

Frederick lived with his mother in a mountain village. The wealthy farmers of the area lived in the valley, working the rich soil and dwelling in substantial stone houses while the poorer people lived on the slopes in log cabins in clearings, often along the edges of the running streams. The poor people had to work hard, cutting wood and growing crops where they could in pockets of rocky soil and watching over their cattle and goats that roamed freely.

Frederick and his mother were poor and they lived in a log cabin. One of the windows looked out over the valley but the other looked towards the higher mountains behind, and in particular, it looked out towards a great face that had been beautifully carved into the rock. From a young age, Frederick was fascinated by the face. He spent hours looking at it, especially when the early evening sun cast beams of light across it and when it was first lit at dawn. Many times he asked his mother who had carved it and how long it had been there. She asked others but always the answer was that no one knew. It had just always been there as long as anyone remembered.

Old Janet fingered her long grey plait, and said there was a story but she could not remember it. The face was kind and Frederick liked to think of it as a wise father to him. His real father had died before Frederick was able to form memories of him and, on occasion, Frederick's mother would hear him addressing the face as if it was his father.

'Sorry son, your father wasn't like the face,' his mother once said sadly. But she would say no more. And that did not stop young Frederick talking to the face as if it was listening and as if it was wise and kind.

When he was a little older, Frederick joined other children of the village and roamed about and climbed the mountain slopes. Their explorations led them to the rocky outcrop from which the face was carved, and they dared each other to climb it. Frederick was a quiet boy and at first he hung back, partly because of his feelings towards the face, but soon he was being challenged.

'Go on, Frederick, the face has a tickle. Scratch its nose. I dare you.'

Frederick was good at climbing and managed to climb down the forehead and eyes easily, then he slid down the nose and to the cheers from his friends, he made a comic gesture of scratching it. He started to climb up the face, but when he reached the eyebrow, a stone came loose from above the forehead. It rolled past Frederick and lodged firmly in the flare of the nostril.

At home, Frederick still gazed at the face, now with a little bump by one side of the nose.

'Mother, I wish the face would really speak to me,' he said one day as the two were sitting on the bench in the late afternoon sun. 'He would say such wise things.'

'I meant to tell you – Old Janet has recalled the story attached to the face,' she said. 'They say that one day a man born in the village will be here, and because of the good ways in which he has led his life, his face will become like the face in the rock, one of wisdom and kindness.'

Frederick became determined to meet that man.

Time went on. Frederick grew up working hard. Most of his friends left the village and went to the big town to work and set up families, but Frederick would not leave his mother who was becoming frail. In the time he spent with her, she taught him to read and write so he could manage on his own. He would do odd jobs for others whose children had left the village and who now needed help. He would get in extra wood when the snows came, feed the animals, seek out the odd cow that had wandered too far on the slopes. He still looked up to the face but it seemed now to have changed from a father figure, to a wise teacher.

Then near to a Christmas, there was talk of a wealthy businessman coming back to the village to build himself a grand house on the mountainside. He was the boy who had dared Frederick to climb down the face but now this man was famous. He owned ships that traded all over the world and brought many luxuries, furs, chocolate and new wines to the ports of North America. The villagers came out to greet him. Frederick thought, surely this must be the man for whom he waited, the man who would have a face like the face on the rocky cliff. When he tried to remember the man's face when he was a boy, he could imagine how it could be transformed.

He started to climb up the face, but when he reached the eyebrow, a stone came loose from above the forehead and lodged firmly in the flare of the nostril.

The carriage drawn by four fine greys galloped into the village. Frederick could hardly see the figure inside. The figure did not acknowledge the waves of the villagers. The coachman drove straight to the site of the proposed grand house. Frederick was concerned because several of the log cabins belonging to poor people were on that land, so he followed the carriage through the valley and up the mountainside. There was the man arrogantly pacing around the land, arguing and waving his fists at three villagers whose cabins were in his way. His face was nothing like that of the face on the mountain. The man built his grand house, and Frederick led several villagers in helping three sad people to move their cabins and rebuild them on the more sloping ground nearby.

Then there was talk of another man returning to the village. He was also famous but his talent had been in military life. He had fought in many campaigns and had been decorated for his bravery. Frederick remembered him as well. As a boy he was always one of the bravest. The wealthy farmhouses in the valley were decorated and flags were flown to welcome him back. Maybe he would be the face on the mountain. Surely, to lead men to success in battle must require wisdom and will and at least a concern for his troops. The half-remembered face in Frederick's mind could also look like the face on the cliff. But the man who arrived and enjoyed the pomp and celebration lavished on him was hardened and spoke in a demanding, commanding manner. There was no humanity left.

Frederick was old now, but still working, still making people smile, still there to help those in need. And when a poet was said to be returning to the village, Frederick renewed his hopes yet again that this would be the man for whom he waited. A poet surely would have wisdom and humanity. Would this be the dream fulfilled? Frederick read the works of the poet and went to meet him when he arrived. He was a lovely man and they talked for hours and walked together. Frederick kept wondering if the man's face matched that of the face on the rock. He half believed it did. One day they walked up the mountain to the land below the great face and Frederick told the poet of his dream. The poet turned.

'I cannot fulfil your dream. This face in the cliff is not mine. I have not been kind to those I have been with. Before the poetry came, I indulged in an ignoble life of drink and debauchery.'

Frederick sighed and there were tears in the eyes of the poet.

Two weeks later, Frederick arranged that the poet should read some of his works at sunset after the people had finished their work. People gathered on the green space beneath the face. As he walked up the track to the place, Frederick picked some flowers to give to the poet as a thank you. He stood and listened to the poems. The words moved him. But the moment was upset by a bee buzzing round the flowers. Frederick bent to put the flowers down but in so doing was stung just by his nostril. He had no wish to disturb the beautiful words of the poet and went on listening. The site of the sting on his face swelled.

As the poet was reading a poem about beauty, a beam of the fading sun cast across Frederick and across the face in the rock. The poet raised his eyes, saw Frederick, saw the face in the rock and lifted his arm.

'My poem might have been about beauty, but there is the man with the face of beautiful wisdom and kindness,' he said. 'Look, there in your midst.'

Frederick lowered his face in embarrassment. The swelling from the sting matched the stone that had fallen all those years ago. Everyone could see the resemblance.

'Not me,' Frederick said. 'I am of no significance. I am just a villager like you all. There will be a wiser and greater man than me, yet to come.' He paused and lifted his head, 'and as we wait for the man, the face in the rock will continue to remind us of kindness and wisdom.'

The Rock called Lorelei

This is one of the better known folk tales in this book. I have tended to focus on lesser-known stories but this one is so centred around a rock (called Lorelei) that I felt it should be included. Lorelei is a great slab of slate rock on the bank of the river Rhine at Sankt Goarshausen in Germany. Its steep face rears up 132m above the sharp bend in the river.

There are many different versions of the story and writers, poets and musicians have found inspiration in the rock itself and in the myths that have developed around it. The original myth may have derived from the writings of Clemens Brentano, who wrote a novel in 1801. My version picks from several sources including Fairyland (https://myfairyland. jimdo.com) and Wikipedia. Geraldine McCaughrean wrote a version that she called 'The Singer above the River' (1999).

Long before anyone had named the Great Rock there was a girl called Lorelei who was a beauty beyond all other beauties. Her hair flowed like the ever-changing currents in the water; indeed, some said she was the daughter of old Father Rhine. She desired a lover and would stand below the rock on the bend of the river and comb her hair, waiting. Many a boatman steered towards her, blind with passion, and would come to grief in the swirling torrents because he was not the one for whom she waited.

One day there was a man fishing on the far bank. He had dark hair, swarthy looks and a smile that called Cupid into action. Lorelei sung out across the river, calling him to her, and the man could not help himself. He rowed across the waters and she reached out for him. For weeks their love flourished. She helped him to fish, and he played with her long hair, plaiting it and coiling it around his hands. He selected the delicacies of fish that she best loved to eat, and he fed her with gentle fingers. However, one day when he said he had gone fishing, Lorelei noticed that he had landed on the bank opposite and, half-hidden behind a rock, he was talking with – nay even embracing! – a young girl. The siren raged, for in all reality, a siren is what Lorelei was. She could not tolerate her jealousy and when the man rowed back across to her later in the day, she grasped him, screaming so all the world could hear, and dragged him down into the water. Maybe she thought he would now be trapped in her underwater abode for ever. Sadly for her, as a mortal, he drowned.

The siren had chosen to drown her lover to cure her stabbing jealousy, but that left her love unassuaged. She stayed with the body of her lover or roamed up and down the riverside, pouring out the deep and eerie sound of the pain. She could tolerate no one near her and when the boatmen rowed towards her song, thinking that they alone could ease her pain, she tossed her head, shook her long hair and currents of water would suddenly flow, turning boats over or pushing them away from her. But pushing the men away did not help her in her lonely misery either. In this time, no one actually saw her.

One day, in a renewed fit of fury, Lorelei took to climbing the Great Rock. Now at sunrise and sunset, she would stand up so that all around could see her lit by the rays of the rising and dying sun and she would sing out across the river, scattering her songs of longing and pain in the winding and twisting currents. Now Lorelei was visible again in all her beauty, people came from far and wide to gaze across the river at her. And many a man, married or unmarried, felt surely that he could negotiate the currents to reach the shore and scale the slant of the rock to reach her to wrap her in his arms and to teach the siren to fall into utter love for him alone. Many

Now Lorelei was visible again in all her beauty, people came from far and wide to gaze across the river at her.

a man lost his life trying to reach the rock, for from the top, with a flick of her hair, Lorelei could set in motion treacherous whirlpools.

News of the happenings on the River Rhine came to the ears of Count Ludwig of Palatine and his son, the Prince. The danger of that part of the Rhine was interfering with their trading activities. Besides, the Prince loved a challenge and also he was under some political pressure to find a wife. Marriage with this famously beautiful woman would be perfect and everyone would respect him for his bravery in rescuing her, for rescuing her is what he decided he would be doing. He arrived at the quay on the opposite bank of the river and wandered among the boatmen, seeking to select one who would row for him in return for a handful of gold coins.

A young man, Hans, hearing of the offer, came to the quay. Foolishly he had gambled himself into serious debt and needed to pay it off. He lived on the north coast of Germany and had regularly overcome wild storms at sea. The River Rhine would be no challenge. He met with the Prince and the deal was struck. The next morning in darkness they set off to row across the river. Hans was under oath to keep his back to the rock in case he too should fall in love. Slowly the sun rose and Lorelei emerged from the shadows of night, golden light spangling from the white of her gown. Seeing the small boat, she sung out, at first inveigling the Prince, imploring him to come to her; luring him closer.

'Hans, row harder. I can see her. Ah – her beauty. Row harder, harder, Hans.'

Lorelei looked down on the lovestruck Prince, no less angry with a prince than any other man. She tossed her hair and the currents carried the small boat towards the rock but then she drew in other currents. The waters became more turbulent, then there were overfalls and the water boiled in turmoil. The Prince hung on as the boat crashed and reared, but he could not take his eyes from Lorelei.

'I'm coming to you. Wait for me. Lorelei, I'm coming.'

Hans did his best. They were nearing the shore beneath the rock but it was rocky. The little boat rose and crashed down on an outlying rock, turned turtle and was matchsticks in seconds. The two men washed into the heaving waves.

The Count of Palatine was devastated at the death of his son. And he was upset about all the others, too, and the matters of his trade.

'I stand for this no more,' he said, stamping his foot. He called up his men. They were hard, fierce men who had fought many times. He directed them that they should not return for their wages unless they had defeated the siren of the Rhine and made safe that part of the river. Two nights later, in darkness, armed men surrounded Lorelei, many in small boats. They came towards the rock from left and right and straight across. They came in from the land behind. They were men used to climbing rock. As dawn broke and Lorelei began to appear, all the men reached in their pockets for blindfolds and then felt their way forward. Lorelei emerged in full, beautiful as ever. She looked round and seeing all the men climbing towards her, she laughed a great laugh, and her laugh echoed off the rocks. She sung out to them, but still they climbed, unperturbed by her appearance. Then, it seems, she saw that she was beaten. She ran to the edge of the rock and took a great leap into the air. She landed in the river, never to be seen again and never again to bother the boatmen of the Rhine.

The rock, Lorelei, was named after her.

Cherry and the Stone People

The story below has been retold many times but an early reference is Hunt, R. (1881). It is set in Zennor, a small coastal village on the tip of the Cornish peninsula in England. As a village, it is quite isolated now, and would have been more isolated at the time in which the story is set.

Not only has the story been told many times, but there are different speculations as to its meaning. I have included it here initially because it is one of the stories that involves the transformation of live people into stone. It is also a story rich with images and folklore and it works well as a tale with a good beginning, middle and end. In terms of meaning, it could have been a warning to young girls who became house servants, of the potential predation of the masters of the households in which they worked, a common hazard for many centuries. On the other hand, it could also be a story about strangers, strange places, fairies and the unknown.

I have adapted the story and I have softened the sexual innuendoes. I make a few more comments at the end.

Cherry was one of a family of six children. The family scraped a living in a two-roomed cottage near the cliffs of Zennor, in the far west of Cornwall. In winter, wet winds howled round the grey cottage but the summer sun lifted the colours of bright rocks, cliff flowers and wiry grasses. Autumn was the time of the gorse and heather.

The family worked hard on their patch of land. Potatoes usually grew well there. But they could afford no animals. Other families about them had goats. So the only meat the family ate was the occasional fish or foraged shellfish, and they had to chew hard on the meat of the limpets.

But as a family they were happy. A particular treat was the visits of the travelling storyteller who brought news from other places, but also captivated the villagers with his stories. Many of the stories were of the little people. Knowing what tricks the little people could be up to was wise. One story that gripped Cherry was the one in which a lost man was turned into stone because he did not believe in the little people.

Cherry was a lively child, running the cliff paths, teasing the boy who came to collect corn for the mill. But children change. Cherry wanted to do the things her friends did, such as going to Morva Fair, showing off their clothes and meeting sweethearts. There was no money for new clothes or even to buy ribbons and trinkets and sweetmeats at the fair. Cherry skulked around, miserable and cross, and came to admit that the only escape was to go into service. Eleanor, her friend, had done that and came back last month with a smile on her face, wearing a fine frock, telling of a nice boy.

Cherry's mother set about making arrangements for her to work locally. 'If you're in Towednack, then you can come home at weekends,' she said.

But Cherry wanted the money she might earn further east, on the other side of the Downs. She still might try to come home sometimes, she said.

Plied with warnings of the dangers for young girls, Cherry set out, a small bundle on her back and a crust in her pocket. She climbed the road to the higher ground and soon she had gone further than she had ever travelled before. She looked out across the heathland to the fringe of sea and offshore rocks. Her step had been jaunty, but now the realisation of what she was doing hit her. She sat on a milestone. She had rarely spent time alone and now, at the crossroads at Lady Down, she was really alone. Tears came. She could go back. She might go back;

maybe Towednack was a good idea. As she lifted her head there was the sound of horse hooves and a shadow drove across her. A handsome man dressed in a fine black cloak looked down. He greeted her, then apparently seeing the tears in her eyes, asked where she was going.

'Zennor,' she said. 'I set out to find service, but I have lost heart. I go home.'

'What luck,' he said. 'I am on my way to Towednack to find a girl to work for me.' He told her how he was recently widowed and had a young son who needed to be looked after. 'So what about working for me?' He seemed friendly and his smile was enticing.

Better than going home again, Cherry thought and shyly she nodded. 'I'll work for you, Sir.'

'Come then.' He dismounted and led his horse. Cherry felt proud to be walking with such a fine man. They crossed the Downs then walked on green lanes, with hedges nearly meeting overhead and there were meadows with more flowers than Cherry had ever seen. They turned this way and that and Cherry lost sense of time and direction. Then it was growing dark and they came down a steep valley to a ford. The clear stream ran fast across pebbles and the man bent to her and lifted her over the water. By now Cherry was smitten with new feelings and was more excited than ever before.

'We are here.' The man was opening a grand gate. 'My home.'

They went through the gate into a garden. No one had gardens in Zennor. All Cherry knew of gardens were those described in the stories of the storyteller and most of those were enchanted gardens. This was so beautiful. There were flowers of deep red, royal blue, white and yellow round a green lawn that led down to the stream. Birds flew in the sky and there was a strange light, a golden glow but no sign of the sun. The glow lit the frontage of an elegant cottage and near the door was a striking arrangement of strangely shaped stones. They were overhung by trees of red apples and blue plums. Sweet perfume pervaded the air.

Cherry's enchantment was interrupted by the voice of a child. A little boy ran towards them.

'Papa,' he cried. 'Papa.' It was difficult to tell how old he was – three, perhaps – but then there was a look about him. His eyes looked to the other side of her, his expression was of knowing … something?

Then there was a woman standing next to him. She grabbed the child by his shoulder and pushed him towards the house.

'Back inside here, boy,' she said. Then she turned to Cherry and gave her a look of dislike.

Almost too quickly, the Master touched Cherry on the arm.

'Aunt Prudence. This is Aunt Prudence. She's been looking after the boy until I got someone else. My wife's grandmother.' He looked directly at Prudence. 'She is utterly unlike my dear, sweet wife. Prudence will stay only until you know what you are doing. Come.'

Prudence tossed her head, tossing away his words and the Master now moved towards the house. Cherry could hardly draw her eyes from the glory of the garden in this strange twilight. Inside, Prudence had laid out a supper such as that of Cherry's dreams; meats and cheeses, fresh bread and fruit. She moved around, saying nothing but whenever her eyes crossed Cherry's, she glared. They ate and the Master departed. Prudence told Cherry to follow her.

'There are things, girl, you must know', she said, opening the door to a small room. In the room were two mattresses, one smaller than the other, and space for little else. 'You sleep here and the boy there. At night, whether you sleep or not, whether he sleeps or not, you do not open your eyes, and you say nothing. You hear me, girl?'

The look was there again.

'You hear me? Say you understand, girl.' Her fingers gripped on Cherry's arm.

'I understand.' Cherry pulled back.

'At dawn, you take the boy to the pool by the spring in the garden. Wash him. By the spring, there is a stone statue and behind that, a pot of ointment. Put that on his eyes and wash the ointment clean off your hands. You listening to me, girl?' Her grip tightened. 'Then milk the cow. Take a bucket of milk and put the last of it into the bowl you will find by the statue. This is the boy's breakfast. You then come in to do your work here.' She stepped towards Cherry. 'And I warn you, girl, go nowhere else in the house – this room and the kitchen only. Try no other door.'

The next morning Cherry woke, helped the boy to dress and, again belying his years, he led her to the spring. She washed him and looked to the statue; a head and shoulders only, but it looked so real. She found the ointment and when she had anointed the boy's eyes, and washed her hands, turned to call the cow. A beautiful cow was ambling up the lawn, the light reflecting from her red brown coat. Cherry had only once before watched a cow be milked, but the cow stood in front of her and as soon as she touched the teats, milk streamed into the bucket and then the bowl. The boy grabbed at the bowl and drank the milk. Then they went into the house. Prudence was there, still completely unsmiling. She sent the boy off into the garden and instructed Cherry to scald the milk and make butter, then clean the platters and bowls with gard (sandy gravel). Then there was other cleaning. Prudence sat with her knitting, grumbling incoherently and relentlessly watching Cherry's every move.

A few days passed. Cherry had learned what she was expected to do and Prudence remained angry with everyone.

Her anger seemed to increase when the Master asked Cherry to come and help him in the garden. Such relief it was for Cherry to be outside, weeding the parsnips and onions, picking large pears and blue plums. And so pleasant it was to feel the Master smile at her and thank her for her work. One day he held her hand as they walked into the house. This seemed to incur fury in Prudence and afterwards Cherry heard their loud voices in conflict.

Maybe it was connected with this row that the following day, when Cherry came in from milking the cow, instead of shoving the duster into her hand, Prudence demanded that Cherry should take off her shoes. Then without saying a further word, Prudence pulled her by the hand towards a door at the back from the kitchen and with a large key, unlocked it. Cherry hesitated but Prudence drew her into a dark passageway beyond. There was a smell of herbs and earth. They reached another door and Prudence shuffled through the keys, opened the door and pushed Cherry inside. It was cold and a faint blue light seemed to emanate from the floor. It lit stone statues, hundreds of statues that seemed to be marching towards Cherry. They were so real. Cherry recoiled but Prudence pushed her further into the room. Now she saw that many of the statues were incomplete, arms missing, torsos without limbs – all frozen in stone like the figure by the spring. Now Cherry was sure of the danger she was in. Any moment she might be turned into a stone stature, for ever to be in this blue cold room.

'Take me back, take me back,' she said.

Prudence promptly slapped her cold hand across Cherry's mouth, grabbed her dress and pulled her to another door. Again it was locked. The smell was now of old wood. Inside the barely lit room was a large chest like a coffin on legs. It took up most of the room. Prudence produced a cloth and wax and indicated

Stone statues, hundreds of statues that seemed to be marching towards Cherry ...

that Cherry should clean the wood. And, as she had done on the previous days, Prudence pulled her knitting from the depths of her gown and knitted, watching Cherry as she polished the chest. Prudence indicated that she had not polished sufficiently, so Cherry worked on the wood again, but Prudence was not satisfied. This went on and on until suddenly there was a great moan that seemed to flood through the whole room. Cherry thought of the stone figures, pulled back from the box and tripped, collapsing on the stone floor. Prudence stood and for the first time, she laughed with a loud and cruel laugh. But then the other door to the room burst open and the Master was standing there, fury on his face, fury directed at Prudence.

'Bringing the girl in here – how dare you? Leave!' he said.

He picked up Cherry and with kind arms, carried her into the kitchen and gave her warm milk.

Cherry saw no more of Prudence from that day and strangely remembered little of what had happened, except that she feared whatever it was that lurked in the locked rooms, though each morning the statue by the spring reminded her of the stone figures. She might have left this place, but she had no idea how to find her way home. There were some compensations too; now she was mistress of the household. She got on well with the boy but much more so, loved the times when she worked with the Master in the garden and the warm hug and kiss he gave her in thanks.

Time passed. It should have been winter, but the flowers continued to flower, the cow continued to give milk and the spring continued to trickle. The sky was always the same; no sun, but always in the daytime there was that golden light. Cherry was now completely enthralled by the Master. She tried not to think about the locked rooms. Probably she was in the land of Little People, she knew that, but surely the Master at least was human.

Then things changed. The Master began to go away, at first overnight, then for longer. He seemed distant from her on his return and would disappear with few words into the locked rooms. Then she thought she could hear him talking in there. Was he talking with the stone people in the blue light? In the times when the Master was not friendly, she allowed herself to wonder if he was one of the Little People and this increased her unease. She wondered too about the boy; why he remained a small child, apparently not growing up. She wondered about the ointment she put in his eyes each day. It seemed to change him from a sleepy 3-year-old to the odd all-knowing being that he would be until night-time.

There was a day when Cherry felt listless and tired, having worked hard in the garden the day before. She wondered what would happen if she used the ointment. She thought hard about it, then, instead of washing her hands after anointing the boys' eyes, she smeared a little into her eyes. For a moment there was an intense feeling of burning. Cherry reached into the spring to try to wash the stuff from her eyes, but to no avail. Then the burning eased and she looked again into the waters of the pool. No longer was there simply the waving of water weeds, but there was a myriad of people: small men and women, moving around, playing, talking. And there was the Master. Cherry was utterly shocked, seeing him there. She walked back towards the house – and now in the trees, by the flowers, walking on the lawn, were Little People: carrying shopping, walking with sticks, nodding their heads in conversation, going about their business.

Over the next few days the Master was out. He hardly seemed to notice Cherry when he came in. He swept past her, unlocked the door and disappeared. Was it music and laughter that she could hear from the room – or her imagination? Cherry felt hurt and jealous of the other life he apparently led. Then she was clear that there was music and laughter. Cherry crept out-side, and anointed her eyes again, waited for the burning to cease, bent down and looked through the keyhole. Inside the room were Little People, dressed as if for a ball. The Master and a beautiful lady were standing on the coffin, hand in hand with hundreds of others all around, dressed in silks and satins, while the other men wore handsome cloaks. Then Cherry saw the Master pull the lady towards him and kiss her. Cherry pulled herself away and went to bed but did not sleep.

The next day the Master stayed at the house.

'Come and help me in the garden, Cherry,' he said.

She raked and hoed and weeded then picked the peas and beans.

'Thank you, Cherry. You have worked hard.' The Master drew her towards him for a hug and thank you kiss but Cherry pulled back and slapped him hard on the face.

'Go kiss your Little Ladies and tease me no more,' she said, walking off, her emotions stinging.

Later the Master came into the house. He said that now sadly he must ask her to leave. 'As sad also is that I must ask Prudence to come back.'

The next day, Prudence was back, full of smiles and waves. The Master and Cherry closed the garden gate. The Master led his horse, walking beside Cherry in silence. They crossed the ford and walked the deep lanes, turning left and right and bending round fields on stony tracks. After a steep climb, they were at Lady Down crossroads.

'I am sad to leave you here, Cherry. You are a good girl. Be here five days after full Moon in any month and I pass this way. I would want to see you again.'

At home, Cherry's parents had never expected to see her again, and were overjoyed, but Cherry was sad. Though she was angry with him, she bitterly missed the Master. It is said that soon she worked again at Towednack and that she never married, though the Miller's son asked her often. And people knew that soon after there was a new Moon, Cherry would disappear for a day or more somewhere on the Downs, but no one knew what she was doing there.

There seem to be a number of elements of the story that are not fully developed – for example, the idea that Cherry is quite a 'tomboy' and 'full of frolic and mischief' (Hunt, 1881). Sadly, her experience with the Master seems to have beaten the assertive element out of her in the story. There is also mystery round the role of Aunt Prudence and what motivated her emotions – and the stone figures. Was Cherry in danger of joining them? Had they been real people and how were they used by the Little People? But maybe it was wise that Cherry did not ask questions. Maybe it is important that I, too, curb my curiosity.

5

ENVIRONMENTS OF ROCK AND STONE

Rock and stone are cliffs and caves, tunnels and volcanoes. Their influences bear down on the people around them, influencing what they do, how they live, where they can go and what frightens them.

Jack Tries Smuggling

As a storyteller I have come across a number of 'Jack' stories. Often these are introduced through the association with Jack in the 'Jack and the Beanstalk' fairy tale. I wrote this light-hearted story for a session with the Jurassic Coast Trust (associated with the World Heritage site) and it needed the theme of the rocks and the coast. It could have been fictionally located at many places along the Jurassic Coast (East Devon to West Dorset, UK), or cliffs anywhere. The story relies on some real history relating to the behaviour and tricks of smugglers and excise men in the eighteenth and nineteenth centuries.

You will have heard of Jack and his mother and the beanstalk, the giant and the golden goose that laid the golden egg. Well this story is about the same Jack seven years later. While the goose was producing wonderful golden eggs, Jack and his mother moved into the Manor House and lived a rich life. But the goose stopped laying and they had to move back into their old cottage. Jack had never needed to work and didn't really know how to. He wasn't always the brightest of lads, but he had his moments, as you will see. However, there came a day when his mother took Jack by the shoulder and told him that it was time to go out and get a job. Jack nodded. She had said this before, but the hand on his shoulder this time was firm.

'Good and honest work, mind,' she said.

'Good and honest, I'll remember that.'

Next day, with a pack on his back, Jack set out. He went from village to village asking for work. He walked from harbour to harbour along the coast. He walked all day, looked all day. Nothing. Then, at twilight, two men passed him. They had somewhat shabby clothes but they had good round bellies.

'Hello lad. Where are you off to? Long way to the next village this time of night.'

'I'm looking for good and honest work,' Jack told them.

The men looked at each other.

'Maybe we could find you something good and honest,' one said. They laughed. 'You good at climbing cliffs?'

'Climbed a beanstalk once.'

'Good at carrying things?'

'Carried the golden goose down the beanstalk.'

'Can you row?'

'I rowed across the village duck pond once.'

'Right, come back with us. I'm Sam, this is William. We'll see what we can do that's good and honest – eh.'

They went to a nearby cottage and the men disappeared into the back parlour, leaving Jack in the kitchen. There was bread and cheese lying around and he helped himself, then he sat by the warm hearth and fell into a doze.

The men came back a while later, waking Jack with their banter and clattering tankards.

'Yes, you can help us,' said William. 'There be three nights of work. If you succeed there'll be a reward and more work. If not … if not,' He looked at Sam. 'If not – well our friend Ratsy will be taking take care of your entertainment for a while.' He and Sam raised their tankards to each other.

Jack was still trying to wake up. Sam looked at him, suddenly serious.

'Listen boy. Take this lantern but don't light it.' He lifted a lantern from the table. 'Walk up the cliff path. At the top there's Grey Rock, just after there's a path down to the bay and twenty paces on there's Flat Rock. Wait there. Round midnight a three-master ship'll come round the point. If the moon's up you'll see two boats go out to meet it. Now if you see anyone coming along the path, light the lamp, and swing it round you so it flashes out to sea. Do that for a few minutes, then hide and don't move until the coast is clear. It'll be Ratsy the Revenue. If he's around, the casks'll have to go in the caves, if not they come back to the quay. Ratsy's nose is twitching at the moment and 'e know we have work. Be back tomorrow.' Sam grabbed at Jack's collar and stared him in the eyes. 'Got it, boy?'

Jack tried to pull back but he couldn't.

'Remember. No light unless you see the Revenue. And if you do see him, make sure you hide well.'

At twilight Jack walked to the quay and up the cliff path. The lamp swung from his belt and he felt very professional. He said hello to several villagers. Noticing his lamp, they nodded knowingly. Trees overhung the rocky track as he walked up onto the cliff. It was dark. 'But, no lamp until I see the Revenue,' he reminded himself.

He reached Grey Rock and the path and then Flat Rock. He sat. It was not cold but he huddled in his coat. It was tiring waiting for the hours to pass and soon he dozed, woke and there was nothing to see so he dozed again. Then he woke suddenly. A man in a dark blue jacket was looking down on him from a large horse.

'What are you doing here, lad?'

'Oh – waiting to see if anyone came along but I went to sleep. I was having a dream. I always tell my mum my dreams. Do you want to hear?' Jack started. 'I was looking for a good and honest job and I met some men and I had to ... Oh, maybe it wasn't a dream. I'm a bit chilly.'

'No time for dreams. If you're lost you can follow me down the path to the quay. See you've got a lantern, you'll need it. They call me Ratsy, by the way. Work for His Majesty.'

'Not sure I know how to light the lantern.'

Ratsy helped Jack with the lantern, then set off ahead of him. Jack couldn't keep up but with the light he could find his way down. Through the trees, the light flashed intermittently out to sea and, seeing it, the men out there landed the casks in the caves. Jack reached the quay, long after Ratsy got there and he found an upturned rowing boat and snuggled into some fishy nets for the rest of the night.

The next day he went to William's cottage. William's wife opened the door.

'Thems through 'ere', she said, leading him into the kitchen. The two smugglers sat there, drink in their hands like the night before. William spoke.

'You did what we said, boy. Ratsy was on the prowl as we thought. We saw your flashing light and ran the casks to the caves.'

He took a loud mouthful from his tankard. 'Tonight, go to Grey Rock and take the path down to the bay. Round the bay, there's a cave entrance. Casks are in there. Reverend Bellyver wants one quickly. He's – err, *entertaining* tonight. Keep him in the brandy and we get to use the crypt for some of our *religious purposes*.' William and Sam hunched their shoulders and launched into deep laughter. Jack was about to ask what they meant – but didn't.

'Go to the bay,' continued William. 'Wait until an hour after high tide and bring one cask from the cave up the cliff. Them's heavy but you said you carried a goose. Casks don't wriggle, do they Sam?' Ale slopped down William's smock as he joked. 'If you hear anyone about, hide. Take the cask to the back door of the Rectory. Just inside there'll be an empty cask. Take tha'un to the crypt. Keep in the shadow of the gravestones and the old yew. Ratsy been smelling the goings-on round the church lately. Wouldn't be wanting to let him know he's right, now, would we?' He turned to Sam. 'Now to the serious work,' and he took a long draught from his tankard. 'Be gone, boy.'

Jack made his way to the hidden bay. It was drizzling and he stumbled and slipped down the steep path. He wondered how he would manage when he was carrying a cask. The tide was still too high to get into the cave and he waited for a while then made his way into the cave splashing through the last foot of outgoing water. Once inside the cave, he lit his candle. Casks were neatly stacked at the back, all labelled 'Brandy Francais'. He picked up one and promptly tripped over a rock and fell into the water. It was heavy.

'The Rev would understand if I had a sip, now I'm wet and thirsty and cold,' he thought, and he turned the tap on the cask. The sip turned into a slurp, then another. He lifted up the cask, warmer now and pleased that he had relieved the cask of a small part of its weight.

'Now for the cliff,' he said aloud and started up the narrow path, less steady than he might have been. He did not notice the slow drip from the tap that he had not completely turned off, because everything was wet from the rain. He was halfway up the path when he stopped for a rest. He sat on the cask. Then suddenly Ratsy was staring down at him.

'You again boy? No home and bed to go to?'

'Went for a walk, found this cask to sit on.' Jack's brain sprang into surprising action. 'Just what my mum wants in her cottage, nice little stool, so I'm taking it. Someone must have dropped it.'

'Well we all know who's dropped it.' Ratsy bent over the cask. 'And I'll be having it. Let's see what's in it.' He picked it up. 'Empty. Must have been chucked out. Best French I see. Cask like this could get you into trouble lad. I'll carry it.'

He was halfway up the path when he stopped for a rest. He sat on the cask.

Carrying the cask, Ratsy climbed up to Grey Rock where his horse was tethered, mounted, and balanced the cask on his saddle. Then he led the way down to the quay, Jack following well behind, very grateful that he did not have to carry the cask.

When he got to the quay, Jack found that Ratsy had left the empty cask by the door of the Old Cat and Fiddle Inn and was presumably now drinking with his mates. Jack had an idea – he would change things round a bit. He picked up the empty cask and walked to the church, found his way into the musty crypt, where there were stacks of other casks. He picked up a full one, had another sip and another, and made his way to the Rectory. He left the full one and took the empty one that was waiting for him and hid it in bushes to collect later. He went back to the quay, found the upturned boat and soon was asleep.

Next night, as Jack made his way to William's house, he was thinking of the bag of money he'd get the following day. Then he could go home.

'Yes, lad, Rev Bellyver got his cask,' said William. 'Get this task right and you'll have a reward. But tonight's tough. Ratsy's nose is twitching so hard he nearly wobbles off his horse. Surprised you didn't see him last night.' William sucked in breath and looked at Sam. 'Or he hasn't seen you …' They laughed a deep belly laugh.

'With Ratsy's extra *curiosity* we need to get the other casks to a safer place,' said Sam. 'Lucky you're here to help us. Now listen,' he continued. 'When it's dark, use the black boat at the quay to collect five casks from the cave in the bay. Pull the fishing nets over them in the boat. Just round the point, you'll find Old Joe's lobster pots under the cliffs. Attach the casks to the lines under the floats and send 'em to the bottom.'

'What'll happen to the lobsters in the pots?' said Jack, a little alarmed.

'What's an old lobster beside a cask of best brandy? Now go. Sometimes brains is not helpful, lad.'

Jack collected the casks and rowed round to Joe's pots. The floats were bobbing in the gentle swell. He got one of the casks attached to the line then thought of it landing on the unsuspecting lobster in the lobster pot below. Jack liked animals and, more to the point, his mum loved lobster. 'I'll just get the lobster out first,' he thought. 'Then I can take it home.'

He hauled up the pot but as it broke the surface, it split and a large lobster escaped into the boat, waving great claws at Jack. Now Jack wasn't so sure about this creature. He fended it off with the cask, nearly tipping the boat but eventually he managed to get the net over the scrabbling mass of claw and leg. Now he'd had enough. He threw back the pot then the attached cask and then he threw out the other four casks and rowed for the quay as fast as he could only too aware of the claws that kept appearing through the net.

As he lay beneath the rowing boat that night, with the lobster as far from him as possible, Jack was thinking. Money, a nice cask for a stool, and a lobster. Mum will be so pleased. Though there was the small matter of carrying it all home. He went to sleep imagining lobster claws lengthening towards his face.

The next morning, he marched cheerily up to William's house and knocked. William opened the door.

'All done,' said Jack.

William turned. There was some grunting inside and he came back to the door with a large leather bag.

'Your reward, boy. Only got small change so a big bag. Ratsy is – shall we say – interfering with our earnings at present.'

'A bag! Just what I needed,' said Jack. 'You see I got a lobster and I want to take it home.' He took the bag. 'My mum'll be –'

The door shut firmly, then opened.

'Lobster? Where did that come from?' There was a pause. 'Never mind, boy. Take good and honest opportunities when they come to you.' The door was slammed and there was a roar of drunken laughter.

The bag was heavy with the small change. Jack collected the cask from the bushes by the Rectory, then went to the quay for the lobster that was still netted under the boat, though now passive. He tipped out the coins, took a deep breath and gingerly gripped the lobster from behind and stuffed it into the bag. But what was he going to do with the money? He looked at the cask and pulled at the tap. Out it came suddenly, throwing him backwards. He picked himself up, put the coins into the cask, plugged back the tap and set off, heavily laden but pleased with himself, a pleasure that decreased as he struggled and sweated up the cliff path. He sat, exhausted. He would have to leave something behind and come back for it. Then there were hooves and it was Ratsy again.

'You lad,' he said. 'Seems you got the cask I had from you t'other day.'

'For my mum,' Jack said, 'and I've got a lobster.' He proudly held up the kicking bag. 'But I can't carry it all.'

'Lobster? I'd like lobster for my tea tonight,' said Ratsy. 'Tell you what, I'll do a deal. I'll carry your cask to Seaminster Cross – that helps you, doesn't it? In return you give me the lobster. How about that?'

Jack wanted the lobster but he just could not carry it all.

'All right,' he said, and reluctantly handed the cask, containing his money, to Ratsy.

'It's full,' said Ratsy. 'Well now this is different. I'll have to ask you some questions. Follow me.'

Ratsy rode ahead and Jack walked more and more slowly. Rounding a corner, away from Jack's view, Ratsy fancied that he needed to try the best French Brandy for flavour and he turned the tap. Nothing. He shook the cask and heard the clink of coins.

Ratsy was not waiting for Jack at Seaminster Cross. He had taken the money to his secret stash in another cave. And actually Jack had used his bit of brain and found another route home, thinking it wise to avoid Seaminster Cross. His mother was so overjoyed to see her son return, she did not worry that he had earned nothing. Knowing her son rather well, she had not really expected him to come back with much. And they did enjoy the lobster for tea. And it was not long before Jack went seeking his fortune again – in a good and honest way, of course.

Rice Cakes for Dinner

I first came across the Japanese story 'The Woman and the Rice Cakes' in a collection of 'feminist folk tales' (Phelps 1981) but there are plenty of other references to it online and I have developed other details in my retelling of it. I have told it many times. It works for all ages but the very young. There is great visual and sound imagery to play up and the resolution of the tale is clever. The story involves 'Oni', which are Japanese ogres that have a wonderful appearance and they qualify the story for Halloween tellings too. The tale is set both on a mountain and inside rocky caves deep inside the mountain, and that is its qualification for being in this book.

Long ago in ancient Japan there was an old woman who lived in a village in the mountains. She was very poor and as many others around her, she could only afford to live on rice. Early in the evening she would carefully cook enough rice to make one rice cake and then would sit on the bench by her door and slowly savour this one meal of the day. It was the best moment of the day. Her perfectly round rice cakes were known to be particularly good.

One day as she was lifting the rice cake from the pan over the fire, a fly buzzed round her eyes. She flipped it away and in so doing, she dropped the rice cake from the pan. It landed on its edge and rolled down the track like a cartwheel, bouncing from rock to rock. The woman gathered up the torn rags of her kimono and ran after the cake. Each time she could just reach it and bent to pick it up, it picked up speed, almost as if someone was drawing it down the mountain side. She ran and ran, breathed hard and ran, driven on by pangs of hunger. She was nearly at the bottom of the mountain. Surely here the rice cake would stop rolling. It did. It stopped rolling and fell on its side in the shadow of a great rock. She reached out. She would be eating soon. But from behind the rock something emerged, something with three hairy claws, something that grasped the rice cake and whisked it back behind the rock. The woman knew what the thing was. Everyone knew about oni, though few could claim to have seen one.

Oni live inside the caves and tunnels in the mountains. They are hulking and heavy ogres with a bluish skin and three eyes across their heads, and three (or some people said four) sharp horns growing out through wild brown hair. They are very greedy and to satisfy their greed they conveniently have mouths that extend from ear to ear in their very wide faces. And they have hairy claws at the end of long hairy limbs, as the woman had seen.

Such was her hunger, the woman threw caution to the wind.

'Give me back my rice cake,' she yelled. Nothing happened except that she heard a scuffling noise then a disappearing thumping as the oni retreated. She remembered as a child clambering up this rock and seeing that a cave ran behind it. She clambered up the rock and was so thin that she was able to squeeze into the cave. It was dark but for the faint lights of fireflies that flittered around. The cave led into a tunnel into the mountain and the oni was thumping along ahead of her. She followed, yelling again to the oni, her words echoing on the rock walls.

'My rice cake, please … my only meal … '

The oni was not that quick and she was catching up with its hairy silhouette when it turned into a side tunnel, and then turned again. A thought flickered in her mind – how will I find my way out? But she carried on, still shouting.

Suddenly the oni stopped, lit now by a flood of light and she could see the real ugliness of the creature – except that it was not just one creature now, but there were dozens of oni with their horrible faces screwed into a look of expectancy. They were holding out their hairy arms apparently expecting a piece of her one little rice cake. Seeing the woman arrive in their cave, the oni all set up a strange howl, apparently of delight, that echoed round the walls.

'Please give me back my rice ...' She did not finish what she was saying because the rice cake had disappeared into many of the huge mouths and the oni were smiling with pleasure. Some rubbed their hairy blue-pink stomachs.

'We like,' said the oni that she had followed. 'I Chief.'

'Please give me back my rice ...'

'Well now I will starve, but please, Chief, show me out of the mountain,' she said.

There was a humming sound from all the oni and Chief slowly shook his hairy head. He had a deep voice.

'You make more rice cakes for us.'

The woman sighed but such was the state of her hunger that the idea of making some rice cakes, and maybe getting one to eat for herself, was almost appealing.

'Come,' he said and he beckoned her to follow with his hairy claws.

He lumbered off into another tunnel and she followed. They went left and left and right and left down different tunnels and arrived in another cave. The light of the fireflies reflected in a stream that ran through the cave, in one side and out of another. In the middle of the floor was a fire and over the fire a frame from which to hang a very large pan. The pans themselves were under some shelves and on the shelves sat a small packet that said 'Rice' on it and another that said 'Salt'. Leaning up on the shelves was a large spurtle for stirring rice.

'You make rice cakes here,' said the oni. He was dragging one of the pans to the stream and ladling water into it. He set it above the fire and tipped some salt into the water. Then he took the tiny packet of rice down from the shelf and tipped into the pan a small handful of rice that barely covered the bottom of the pan.

'That's not enough rice,' said the woman.

'Huh,' said the oni with a wry smile on his huge mouth. He took the spurtle and started to stir the mixture. As the water heated and the spurtle stirred, the rice expanded – and expanded – and expanded until there was a full pan of rice.

The woman stood back in amazement.

'Now you make cakes,' said the oni and he turned and left her to the task.

She made dozens of rice cakes, and quickly ate three before a small team of oni arrived to carry the rest back to the large cave. They were eaten with noisy relish and tummy rubbing.

'Now, tell me, how do I get out of this warren?' the woman asked. The oni looked at her with a wide smile.

'You cook for us – forever,' he said.

Horror. To live in this cave with these ugly monsters, forever? The woman just managed not to cry out. Then she thought, 'I will escape, but I need to think how, so I will do what they ask for a day or two and think.'

She thought, and in two days had worked out a plan. She would escape by way of the stream. It was well known that oni do not go into water. She had noticed that the oni went to sleep after their rice cake meal. She could hear their roaring snores echoing through the tunnels. When she heard this on the third day, she put the spurtle into the largest pan and dragged and lifted it to the stream as quietly as she could. She got into it and pushed off. The pan had just started to pick up the current and move downstream where it left the cave when she heard thumping feet. The scraping sound had woken the oni and one by one they paced into the kitchen and lined up along the stream. Without any signal they bent down and with their great big mouths, started to suck up the water. The pan ceased to move forward and bounced on the rocky stream bed, then grounded. The oni went on drinking.

However, as the water got lower something else happened. The fish in the stream started flipping their tails and jumping out of the water. In sheer panic, the woman caught hold of the jumping fish and threw them hard at the oni. The oni now opened their mouths to catch the fish – and as the fish went into their greedy stomachs, the water that they had drunk came out like a fountain. The more fish the woman threw, the more the water was replaced in the stream, and now the pan juddered forward then moved freely again. It drifted towards the tunnel, she ducked her head and she was in darkness but she was being carried out of the mountain. She had to push herself off with the spurtle once or twice but then there was a pinpoint of light, then a flood of light and she was out of the mountain in the full light of day. What relief. She climbed out of the pan and found the track up to her village. The spurtle worked as a good walking stick.

With the activity of the day, the woman was hungry and set about making her rice cake. But to her surprise, when she stirred her few grains of rice with the spurtle, the few grains became more and more and filled her little pan with rice and she was able to make five rice cakes.

The next day she got help to bring the large pan from where she had left it to her village and she started making rice cakes for the whole village. She was never hungry again and was even able to buy a new and very pretty kimono.

The Girl who Learned to Hunt

This story is from the Zuni culture. The Zuni tribe live in what is now New Mexico in the United States of America. Their traditional villages or pueblos comprised stone buildings often linked to caves, or they were built in the shelter of overhanging rock.

I first came across the retold story in Phelps (1981), a collection of 'feminist stories', and I researched it further. I do not consider that this story as written by Phelps is actually feminist. At the end of it, the heroine is helped by two other male characters and she would have failed in the story without their help. In that form, I would not have chosen to tell the story because I did not feel it has a sufficiently strong ending to make a good oral story, so for oral storytelling I modified this part. However, since the story is bound up in its cultural origins, I give both endings – the traditional ending and the modified form. The latter in particular, involves stone and rock, though a landscape of caves and stone is the setting for both.

It was a great tragedy to the family when The Girl's two older brothers were killed in tribal fighting. Many families lost one boy, but to lose both was a terrible loss. The parents were getting older and had relied more and more on the boys to hunt rabbit and deer to provide them with the meat and skins that helped them to survive the long and bitter winters. But now there was only The Girl left.

Among the Zuni, girls did not hunt. This Girl, though, had spent many childhood hours with her bothers, watching them as they learned to throw rabbit sticks, thread the dead rabbits onto strings of yucca for carrying, skin deer and make flint knives to butcher the carcasses to cook and eat. But in the normal course of things she would never do any of this for real. Girls didn't.

When her brothers died, The Girl had to work harder. She sowed maize and beans for the family, grew large orange pumpkins and multicoloured squash. She harvested these and ground the corn to meal and made the cornbread and corn cakes. But there was no meat. If the family was lucky they would be given a little dried meat by others in the pueblo, but this was scarcely enough for one meal. The Girl also had to collect enough wood to keep alive the flames of the fire. Sometimes this was more than she could manage and so they were often cold and they were always hungry. And the winter after the boys died came early. Snow fell and then continued to fall. The family shivered in front of their fire.

The Girl would watch the young men of the pueblo return with strings of rabbit and she wished she could go hunting. She thought about hunting as she collected the firewood and then one day when pangs of hunger were particularly bad, she decided that she would go hunting. She told her parents. They were shocked.

'Girls are not made for hunting,' the father said.

'You would get lost. We would lose you,' the mother said.

But The Girl was determined.

'At the day after full moon, I am starting to hunt,' she announced.

At last she was taken seriously. The parents brought out the buckskin clothing that the brothers had used, shed some more tears over them, and for the next day or two the mother sat by the fire and sewed leggings and a tunic to fit her. On the morning after full moon, The Girl reached for the flint axes that had hung on the wall since the day the boys died, pushed rabbit sticks into her belt and put a handful of corn cakes into a bag over her shoulder.

She set out late so as not to be seen by the other hunters. It had snowed but now the sky was bright. She followed the river up the canyon then took the long track up to the higher ridges. Then she cut across virgin snow to the area of rock, scrub and cacti, to where there were plenty of rabbit tracks in the snow. Rabbits were there but at first she missed most of them with the sticks, but then there were successes; her first rabbit and then more. There were not yet enough, but she was getting more accurate in her throwing. She stalked, ran and crouched, excited that she could hunt. She did not notice the gentle fall of snowflakes that turned heavier; she just pulled the skins further up around her neck. Later on, with ten rabbits on the string, she cleared snow from a red rock and sat to eat her corn cakes.

The Girl was happy with her hunting and it was time to return. She stood, took a step and realised that the snow had obliterated her previous tracks – that she intended to follow. With the heavy clouds rolling in, it was getting dark. She floundered around in the deepening snow, then knew she must do what her brothers had done on occasions: find a cave in which she could rest for the night, and hopefully find some firewood with which to make a fire.

She was lucky. Nearby there were cliffs, and in the cliffs was a tiny entrance to a cave. She cleared one or two rocks and climbed in. Other hunters had obviously been there and had left the remains of a hearth. Outside, under the scrub, she found more wood to burn. She set the fire and pulled out one of the flint knives she always carried and skinned two rabbits, then threaded the meat on sticks and cooked it over the fire. It was the first fresh meat she had eaten for a long time. She prepared another rabbit, then she started to clear stones from a space near the fire so she could sleep. She could see out through the small entrance to the cave that it was nearly dark.

It was then that she heard the first sound. Something was moving through the snow outside. It could be bear or wolf. She was wary of the larger wild animals, but the cave entrance was small, and besides, her fire would ward off most. It might be another hunter who was lost.

'There's a cave here, warm fire,' she called but other than the echo of her voice, there was no human response. She settled down. Then, another sound, a sound that was closer, something heavy tripped over a rock. There was a deep grunt. Looking up she saw that a thing, large and round was silhouetted in the faint light of the cave entrance.

'Food, I smell food,' it growled.

She clutched her axe, terrified. All Zuni knew about strange creatures that roamed the hills, but they never expected to see one. For sure, she was now facing one, an Atahsaia, a giant demon, known to eat anything, including its own kind. It roared again and hit at the cave entrance with a clawed fist, then its hairy and muscular arm reached into the cave.

'Food! Give me rabbit!' it roared.

But it was too large to get in. The Girl sat, unmoving. The Demon pushed its head into the entrance; the red of its eyes, the swollen face and the long grey hair lit horribly by the flickering of her fire. Then there was something more dreadful. The head withdrew and there was a great crack and another, stone on stone. The Atahsaias carried huge flint axes and this one was using the axe to break up the rocks at the entrance to the cave.

'Rabbit first, then girl human,' it roared again as the rocks split and the entrance hole enlarged.

The Girl looked around the cave. There was no escape.

Traditional Zuni ending to this story

Outside in the cold night, however, the sound of the axe on the rocks resounded around the cliffs and canyons and others heard it. The Gods of War and Chance, Ahayuta and Matsailema, heard it and raced through the night air, their war clubs ready. They pulled the hulking Atahsaia from the cave entrance, and clubbed it from behind until it let go. It turned and with stumbling steps, retreated into the night.

'You are safe now, Girl. Sleep now. We will watch over you.'

The Girl slept an exhausted sleep and woke to beams of sunlight coming through the entrance to the cave. She picked up her string of rabbits. Outside the Gods waited for her. They led her to the track that would take her to her pueblo.

'Now be safe,' they said. She turned to acknowledge their kindness, but they were no longer there. She made her way back. The people had heard that she had not returned.

'Shouldn't have let a girl go hunting,' they said, but when they saw her fit and well with her good string of rabbits, they celebrated. Her parents celebrated even more and from then on The Girl hunted regularly, often bringing back enough rabbits to sell, and now the family ate well and her work was easier. When she hunted though, she never allowed her enthusiasm with the rabbit sticks to keep her out in the wild beyond the beginnings of twilight.

A rewritten ending

Outside in the cold night, the sound of the axe on the rocks resounded round the cliffs and canyons. There was rubble on the floor of the cave, and the Girl tried throwing stones at the Demon. His actions continued.

'All right, have a rabbit,' she said, flinging one of the rabbits she had caught.

'All right, have a rabbit,' she said, flinging one of the rabbits she had caught.

The Demon put down his axe and ate the rabbit. She threw another. Again he stopped battering at the entrance while he ate.

'More,' it roared. She threw another, and another. Now the Demon would simply open its mouth and catch the rabbits she threw. She knew she was only holding it off for a short while. Three rabbits were left.

It was then that she had an idea. The two rabbit skins from her meal were drying by the fire. She wrapped a few sharp stones in a skin and threw it. The Demon opened its mouth, caught the rabbit skin and yelped loudly. She could see it clawing at its mouth in pain, snarling through broken teeth, then holding its throat. It had swallowed the stone-filled skin. She stood and threw a large rock that hit it full square on the face and now it turned and she could hear it retreating, grunting and growling with each pace. She looked outside into the cold darkness. It was gone. She stoked the fire, looked sadly at the two rabbits – all that was left from her hunt, and eventually slept.

The Girl was woken by a beam of warm sun. She collected up her things and with the position of the sun as her guide, she recognised her location. There were plenty of rabbits hopping around and as she walked, she threw her stick, determined to make up for the number that had been eaten by the Demon.

The arrival of the Girl back at the pueblo was celebrated. People had thought her lost.

'That's what happens when a girl hunts,' they had said, but now they saw the substantial string of rabbits and the jauntiness of her step, they admitted they might be wrong. From then on The Girl hunted regularly. The family ate well and often there were rabbits left over to sell. However, The Girl held on to her secret. She did not tell anyone what had really happened that night, but nor did the young men tell of their experiences with the demons, and she never allowed her enthusiasm with the rabbit sticks to keep her out in the wild beyond the beginnings of twilight.

Licarayén: a Volcano Myth

I heard this story in a very memorable moment. I was already writing this book and I was on the lookout for a volcano story. I was in a group of cyclists and we were ten minutes into the first day of a cycling holiday in the lake districts of south-west Chile and Argentina in South America. We were in the outskirts of Puerto Varas, starting our ride round the blue waters of Lake Llanquihue. Suddenly there towered over us a tall sculpture of Licarayén, the young girl in the story below. The sculpture raised her hands in the sunlit air to the snow-capped volcano on the opposite side of the lake. This mountain is now called Osorno and is one of the most active volcanoes in South America. The last eruption in the area was in 2015. In the story Osorno is called Piri Pillén Round the sculpture the story is depicted on mosaic tiles. Ali, our guide, then told the story that I have retold below. It relates to the Gods of the Mapuche people of this area of Chile. Antu was the principal Pillan spirit in Mapuche mythology. He represented the sun, light, wisdom and spirit and he was considered to be the opposite to darkness and the physical world.

In the far back mists of time, the Huilliche people lived in a region of high mountains in the south of Chile. Their villages clustered by the water at the foot of the mountain that was called Piri Pillén. Times were good for the people and they were ruled peacefully by a wise Cacique. The Cacique's daughter, Licarayén, was admired as much for her wisdom as for her beauty, and often her father would turn to her for advice and counsel. She was in love with the Toqui, Quitralpique and plans were in place for them to be married at the flowering time of the flame trees, the following spring.

However, the mountain Piri Pillén was angry with the Huilliche people. He was jealous because he had been told that they had been created by Antu, who had then gone on to entrap himself inside the rocky mountain of Piri Pillén, causing the mountain serious belly aches. So in his spite, Piri Pillén was determined to find a way of denying the people their comfortable lives.

One day, when the people were going about their chores, dusting their huts, setting up their market stalls, feeding their animals or tending their corn in the fields, he rattled and shook the ground under their feet. Dogs barked, twigs fell from trees, dust was shaken from the woodwork of huts and people looked at each other in fear. Then they looked down as cracks opened up in the earth and the waters of their streams turned around and flowed the other way or worse, flowed down into the cracks. Over days, there were many quakes. People clustered in groups and talked about what was happening. They slept in the open air and it was cold. But all the time they tried to do their work as usual and tried to keep smiling at each other, and Piri Pillén realised that he was not managing to disrupt their well-being as much as he hoped. So he ramped up his anger and he began to spit fire. Larva poured out of his crown and ran searing red down his valleys. Rock and dust landed everywhere, crushing homes and drowning fields and crops in black grit. The fury was such that no one had ever seen. The Cacique held counsel with all those around but everyone held their hands up, empty of ideas. The suffering continued.

Then one day an old traveller arrived. He had heard of the disaster and requested immediate audience with the Cacique. By then the Cacique was casting around, talking with anyone who might have any idea of how to cure the mountain. The old traveller brought knowledge from other lands. He said that the way to calm the mountain was to make a sacrifice of the most beautiful Huilliche girl. Her heart should be ripped from her body and the Cacique should place it at the top of Pichi Juan hill, in the foothills of Piri Pillén, beneath a frond of the herb fennel.

In his democratic wisdom, the Cacique said that the girl would be chosen by the people. For days, people gathered in the marketplace, discussing their choice, agonising over the decision. At last the news was taken to the Cacique. They had chosen Licarayén.

It was with her usual grace and dignity that Licarayén accepted the choice and agreed to give up her life for her people. But she asked one condition, that it would be her fiancé, Quitralpique, who would take her heart from her body as it was he who now owned her heart.

As they stood back there was a rush of air and a great bird landed, took up the heart in its beak and picked up the herb in its talons.

The ceremony was prepared. In the background, Piri Pillén still roared his fiery fury. Licarayén was laid on a bed of flowers and the sacrifice was made. Without hesitation then, Quitralpique cast himself onto his spear so that he could enter the afterlife with his love.

In the depth of despair and carrying his daughter's heart and the feathery fennel, the Cacique, with a small group of advisors, undertook the terrible journey to Pichi Juan hill. They placed the heart on the summit and waited. As they stood back there was a rush of air and a great bird landed, took up the heart in its beak and picked up the herb in its talons.

The small party watched as the bird flew into fire and flame and into the mouth of Piri Pillén. And as they went on watching, a great purple and grey cloud rose behind the mountain and moved across its summit, scattering its storm of snow. Steam poured from the mountain's mouth, and water began to run like floods of tears down the mountain sides. Battle between the fire anger of the mountain and snow-pure heart of the girl was being fought out.

And at last it was the heart of the girl that won. So much snow had fallen and so much water poured down the mountain that three lakes were formed – Chapo, Lagos Todos Los Santos and Lagos LLanquihue. They exist today. And from then on, the Huilliche people lived for years in relative peace. And in addition, with their new watery landscape they learned the skills of fishing and the arts of cooking fish.

A Tale of Two Walls

This is the retelling of a Chinese folk tale. It is a dark story that I have only told to adults, though the story starts like a fairy story. It is a story of surprises that has a major shift in the middle, and it seems likely that it is two stories that have become melded together. There are some historical facts on which the second part of the story (or the second story) are based and this second part has also been described as 'one of the greatest stories of China'. There is suggestion that this version of the story dates from the nineteenth century.

The wall in the story is not the 'Great Wall of China' as we now know it, but an earlier wall that was constructed by joining up city and state walls and natural boundaries such as river defences. And as the story tells, there may have been difficulties in building it.

The story I retell is based on a book found in a junk shop: a collection of 'fairy stories' from China (Bonnet 1958), which were in turn derived from earlier collections.

The Chiangs and Mengs were neighbouring families who lived in small shacks on the open plains. They decided to construct a wall around each house to fend off the winds that blew fiercely from the north. They laboured with clay, stone and some beautiful tiles for the top of the wall. They had material left over so they built a wall up between the two houses. This was a shame as now they could not talk to each other so easily, but it looked neat and some plants grew upwards in their gardens, no longer bullied by the winds.

It was not unusual that both the Chiangs and the Mengs planted pumpkins that year. And it was not unusual that most pumpkins died except for one plant each and these plants scrambled up the new wall. And when the plants reached the top and lay across the blue tiles they grew together, and out of their growth there came to be one yellow pumpkin. The one pumpkin, sitting on top of the wall, expanded and expanded. The families, watching it from their respective sides, marvelled at its increasing size. They were proud of it, calling out comments to each other, and bringing their friends to see it.

Then it was time to harvest the pumpkin. They decided that the mothers of the families should cut it from the stem and the fathers would divide it in half and each family would have half. A stool was brought out from each shack and the two mothers cut the stem of the pumpkin, then the fathers climbed on their stools to cut it in half. Each had a knife. But they had not put their knives far into the yellow skin when there was a sound.

It was time to harvest the pumpkin. They decided that the mothers of the families should cut it from the stem.

'Please take care with your knives, I am here.'

A young child's voice: the men wobbled and looked round. There were only their young children there and the voice was not theirs. They looked back at the pumpkin and now a small hand pushed out through the flesh of the fruit. Mr Meng fell off his stool in surprise and as he toppled, he pulled the pumpkin with him. He fortunately landed in his wife's arms. The pumpkin hit the ground and split. From the creamy flesh and seeds, a pretty little girl emerged. The Mengs exclaimed in surprise, and a row of Chiang heads appeared over the wall.

The two families decided it was only fair if the girl was brought up by both, so they took down the wall between the houses and she happily ran from one to another set of doting parents. They called her Chiang Meng and she grew up to be an intelligent and beautiful young woman.

At that time in China, a boy grew up to be a great emperor who took pride in his utter cruelty and powerfulness. His name was Chi'in Shih Huang-ti and he was an ambitious and cruel man. He was determined not to let his enemies get the better of him and so when there were uprisings in the north of China, he decided to build a wall to keep them under control. It was to be an enormously long wall.

It might have been the plans for the wall, or the labourers not being up to the task, but as soon as sections of the wall were built, they promptly fell down. The Emperor was infuriated. He imprisoned, he executed, but nothing helped. One day an advisor reported that he had received a divine message – that if for every mile of the wall, the Emperor would kill a man and bury his bones in that part of wall, the wall would stand.

'Yes,' said the Emperor.

When people heard what their vile leader intended there was wailing and crying throughout the land.

The Emperor thought it over. Killing men was easy but organising burials every mile was time-consuming and tedious for a man bent on showing off the thousands of miles of wall to the state dignitaries. Then news came of another minister with another idea. The man was shown into the Emperor's palace and he sidled into the grand throne room, head lowered to his hands and he bowed to the floor.

'Speak on your solution to our problem,' said the Emperor.

'I know a man called Wan,' said the man. 'Bury him in the wall and you will have buried 10,000. The wall will stand firm.'

The word 'Wan' meant '10,000'.

'Yes.' The Emperor pulled his thin lips near to a smile. 'So then bring a man called Wan to me.'

The man Wan heard of his fate and fled from his home, ducking and diving around soldiers hunting for him. People were sorry for him and risked their lives feeding and sheltering him. And in this way he came to the homes of the Chiangs and the Mengs. That night he saw Chiang Meng when she came in from the fields and as soon as their eyes met, they were in love. No longer would Wan flee and within days a wedding was arranged. The wedding feast was set up and the guests were seated around the table with others from nearby villages, raising toasts to the bride and groom, but then the soldiers marched in. Despite Chiang Meng pleading and throwing herself at their feet seeking mercy, they took Wan and carried him to the Emperor. He was killed and his body was quickly taken and buried in the wall.

In deep grief, Chiang Meng travelled to the wall to search for her young husband's bones. She stood on a hill and looked to the right and to the left, and the wall extended to both horizons. Where was Wan buried? How could she know?

The Emperor heard that Wan's new wife was searching for her husband's bones and he ordered that she should be brought to him.

He liked a good supply of young women and if she was as beautiful as people said, maybe she would be the empress he sought.

Chiang Meng was brought to the Palace. When the Emperor saw her, he wanted her. In anger Chiang Meng kicked at the guards and screamed but then, within seconds she realised that she did not care. Nothing mattered now her Wan was dead. And reality hit. She had no choice. What the Emperor wanted, he got – or did he?

She stood firmly in front of him.

'You killed my husband – whom I loved with all my heart. Grant me three wishes that will allow me to celebrate his life and our love, and I will meet your desires and become empress.'

The Emperor just gazed at the beauty of this woman.

She continued, 'First, there will be a great festival for forty-nine days in honour of my husband. Second, during this festival my husband will be buried honourably. You, Emperor, and your ministers will be present. And thirdly, on a river terrace that will be specially built, I will make a sacrifice to my husband.'

The Emperor was mesmerised by this strong woman and his desire grew.

'Your wishes are granted,' he announced.

Wan's body was fetched from the place in the wall during a grand festival that lasted for forty-nine days. People came from far and wide to honour him – or perhaps to lay eyes on this woman who seemed to be able to control the dreadful Emperor. Wan was buried in an emotional ceremony during which his body was cast into the water. Then, dressed ready for her wedding, Chiang Meng climbed up on the decorated river terrace. She turned towards the Emperor and in a strong voice, cursed his evil deeds and took a step forwards and cast herself into the depths of the fast-flowing river.

The Emperor was consumed with fury at her act of self-sacrifice and, waving his great sword, he ordered that her body should be cut into thousands of pieces. But her body was never found and some say that she swims still with Wan, both turned into the silver fish of the river.

The emperor in the story, Ch'in Shih Huang-ti, was known as the 'First Emperor' of China. He was apparently a very cruel man who relentlessly killed and exploited the citizens. He had many concubines and many children (perhaps up to fifty), though it is said that he never took an empress.

BIBLIOGRAPHY

Bonnet, L., *Chinese Fairy Tales*, (London: Frederick Muller, 1958).

Balfour, M., 'Legends of the Lincolnshire Cars Pt III', *Folklore Vol. 2.4* (1891).

Crimmens, P., *Storymaking and Creative Groupwork with Older People*, (London: Jessica Kingsley, 1998).

'Fairyland', myfairyland.jimdo.com

Hart, M., *Dorset and East Devon Landscape and Geology*, (Marlborough: The Crowood Press, 2009).

Hodgson Burnet, F., *The Secret Garden*, (London: Heinemann, 1911).

Hunt, R., *Popular Romances of the West of England*, 3rd edition, (London, 1881).

Jacobs, J., *More English Fairy Tales*, (London: David Nutt, 1893).

Lang, A., *The Crimson Story Book*, (London: Longman's Green and Co., 1903).

McCaughrean, G., *Golden Myths and Legends of the World*, (London: Orion 1999).

Mead, S., *Great Stories from Many Lands*, (London: James Nisbet, 1936).

Miller, M., *A Kist O'Whistles*, (London: Andre Deutsch, 1990).

Moon, J., *Using Story in Higher Education and Professional Development*, (London: Routledge, 2010).

Moon, J., *Devon Boy 1590*, (Devon: Lympstone History Society, 2017).

Muir, R., *The Stones of Britain*, (London: Michael Joseph, 1986).

Phelps, E., *The Maid of the North*, (New York: Holt, Rinehart and Winston, 1981).

Portanova, J., 'The Story of the Common Willow Pattern Plate', *The Family Friend* (1849).

Ransome, A., *Old Peter's Russian Tales*, (Edinburgh: Nelson, 1916).

Schneidau, L., *Botanical Folk Tales of Britain and Ireland*, (Stroud: The History Press, 2018).

Scriven, S., *Fossils of the Jurassic Coast*, (Dorset: The Jurassic Coast Trust 2016).

The Reader's Digest Folklore, Myths and Legends of Britain, (London: The Reader's Digest Association Ltd, 1977).

Tilley, C., *Landscape in the Longue Durée*, (London: UCL Press, 2017).

Society *for*
Storytelling

Since 1993, The Society for Storytelling has championed the ancient art of oral storytelling and its long and honourable history – not just as entertainment, but also in education, health, and inspiring and changing lives. Storytellers, enthusiasts and academics support and are supported by this registered charity to ensure the art is nurtured and developed throughout the UK.

Many activities of the Society are available to all, such as locating storytellers on the Society website, taking part in our annual National Storytelling Week at the start of every February, purchasing our quarterly magazine Storylines, or attending our Annual Gathering – a chance to revel in engaging performances, inspiring workshops, and the company of like-minded people.

You can also become a member of the Society to support the work we do. In return, you receive free access to Storylines, discounted tickets to the Annual Gathering and other storytelling events, the opportunity to join our mentorship scheme for new storytellers, and more. Among our great deals for members is a 30% discount off titles from The History Press.

For more information, including how to join, please visit

www.sfs.org.uk